Carnival of horrors.

She saw heading straight for Boomer, a sharp wicked-looking, pointed metal tip, the kind she'd been so careful not to order. "No," she had told the carnival supply people, "not real darts. We want the other kind, the rubber suction cup-tipped ones. We don't want anyone getting hurt" . . . she *had* said that.

But someone was going to get hurt, anyway.

Eve opened her mouth to scream, knowing it was already too late.

NIGHTMARE HALL

Dark Moon

DIANE HOH

SCHOLASTIC INC.
New York Toronto London Auckland Sydney

No part of this publication may be reproduced in whole or in
part, or stored in a retrieval system, or transmitted in any form
or by any means, electronic, mechanical, photocopying, record-
ing, or otherwise, without written permission of the publisher.
For information regarding permission, write to Scholastic Inc.,
555 Broadway, New York, NY 10012.

ISBN 0-590-25078-7

12 11 10 9 8 7 6 5 4 3 2 1   5 6 7 8 9/9 0/0

Printed in the U.S.A.   01

First Scholastic printing, May 1995

NIGHTMARE HALL

Dark Moon

Prologue

"I hate you!" the teenager cries. The face is scarlet with rage, the eyes dark with fury. "Everyone else is going. Why do you have to be so uptight about everything? You're ruining my life! I wish you would just die!" Sneakered feet whirl, race up the stairs, stomping down upon each riser. The tall, thin figure in jeans and a plaid shirt runs into the bedroom and slams the door, locking it. Hurtling onto the bed, the teenager lies there, face down, furious.

A full moon shines through the window, illuminating the darkness.

The teenager lies prone on the bed for a long time, finally falling asleep, only to be awakened sometime during the night. The head lifts, glancing at a luminescent clock on the bedside table. Quarter past two in the morning.

The moon is now visible through a different window. The figure on the bed rolls over, think-

ing angrily of being forced to miss the best party of the year. At that moment, a thick, dark shadow slides across the round, pale globe, hiding it as effectively as if someone had just drawn a black velvet curtain over it.

The teenager returns to sleep.

And awakens to bright sunshine flooding the room. A breathless hush lies over the house. Something is not normal. Something has happened. Something is wrong.

There are people downstairs, in the living room, in the kitchen, spilling out onto the wide front porch. Relatives. Neighbors. Friends of the family. All are ashen-faced, with stunned, bleak eyes.

Because something has happened. Something is wrong.

Someone has died.

The mother who was wished dead only the evening before, has obliged — by dying.

Dying during the night, of what the teenager learns in a sympathetic whisper from a relative was a "heart attack." Unexpected. Shocking.

But the teenager knows better. There was no heart attack. The heart stopped beating because it was willed to stop. It stopped beating unexpectedly, for no apparent medical reason because someone wished that it would. Wished hard. Wished so hard that the person had sum-

moned up a power they didn't even know they possessed. The power took over and, under the eerie, luminous glow of a full but shadowed moon, made the heart stop beating.

Didn't mean to. Didn't even know about the power.

But it's too late now.

Still . . . so many parties to go to, so much fun to have — and nothing to stop that now. Nothing to get in the way. The father won't. Doesn't care about things like that. Too busy, too preoccupied, never did have anything to say about it. Only her. She was the one who ruined everything.

Won't be ruining anything anymore, will she?

What time did it happen, is the question posed to the father.

He looks stricken. What? Why do you ask? What difference does it make?

What time? the now-motherless teenager insists.

"Two-fifteen," the father answers reluctantly. "She made this terrible sound, as if someone had just pounded her in the chest, and it woke me up. I glanced at the clock as I woke up and saw it was two-fifteen. I tried to revive her, but . . ."

Two-fifteen. The very moment that the dark

shadow had passed over the full moon.

The teenager would think about that later.

Right now, the thing to do was cry and carry on as expected. It wouldn't be good to let people think there weren't any feelings. Everyone has feelings. Even people with special powers.

Powers for good.

Or evil.

Chapter 1

The highway between Salem University and the town of Twin Falls was so congested with traffic, the cars were barely moving.

"It looks like a parking lot," Eve Forsythe said in dismay. Her roommate and best friend, Andrea Coffee, peered impatiently out over the steering wheel, searching for an escape route. "We should have arranged for the parade to start on campus and move into town instead of the other way around," Eve went on. "I was supposed to meet Kevin and the rest of the Founders' Day committee on Fourth Street half an hour ago! Andie, can't you steer around some of these cars?"

"Oh, sure, Eve," Andrea retorted sarcastically, "a fender-bender right now is just the ticket to solve this traffic problem. Anyway," she added after honking in vain several times, "we all agreed at the first committee meeting that it wouldn't make any sense for the parade to move from campus to town. The Founders' Day celebration is mostly taking place on campus. That's where the carnival is set up, right? So that's where the kick-off parade needs to end up."

Eve sighed. "I know. You're right. But who knew that practically everyone on campus would decide to drive into town? It doesn't look like anyone had the brains to take the shuttle, the way Kevin said they would." She glanced out her window and groaned. "And it's going to rain! I can tell. The wind is fierce and that sky is black as death!"

The car inched forward slightly. "I never should have agreed to cochair this committee," Eve murmured, half to herself. She leaned her head back against the seat. Had her long, wavy hair suddenly slipped free of the wide brass barrette pulling it away from her face, it would have draped itself over the tweed upholstery like a dark, silken cape. But Eve never wore her hair loose. Ever. "Having Kevin as cochairman helps, but I know who's going to feel responsible if the celebration falls apart. *I* am!"

"That's because you're the responsible type," Andie said amiably, stepping on the gas again as a gap appeared in front of her. Her freckled hands held the steering wheel lightly, and her mop of tightly curled, burnt-orange hair moved from side to side as she surveyed the long lines of cars boxing her in. "That's why you were elected over everyone else on the committee who wanted to be chairperson. Like me, for instance." She grinned, and the freckles on her cheeks danced. "Chairing this week-long event would look *so* good on the résumé of a future public-relations genius. Especially if this thing is a success."

Eve groaned. "And what if it isn't? What if the whole thing's a huge disaster? Would you want it on your résumé then?"

Andie shook her head, her grin spreading wider. "Nope. That's why I didn't scream and tear my hair out when you and Kevin were picked over me as chairpersons. I figure, as just one more member of this committee, if things go okay, I can take part of the credit. But if it flops, I'm free and clear. All the blame goes to *you*." She glanced sideways at Eve. "Why are you so jittery? You've organized tons of things. We all know that. Rumor has it that you've never fallen down on the job in your life."

Eve laughed without humor. Andie's earlier comment had stung. "The responsible type?" It made Eve sound so . . . dull. "Right. You know what they say," she said in a brittle voice.

"If you want anything done right, get Eve Forsythe to do it."

It wasn't as if Andie was wrong. She wasn't. Eve *was* more organized than most people. Did that make her dull? Well, maybe she *looked* dull, which could be why she hadn't dated very much since she arrived on Salem's campus. Could be the neatness that scared guys away. She was very neat. Impeccably neat. Her clothes were always clean and pressed, every skirt matched every sweater, her hair was always carefully restrained, and she was obsessive about flossing thoroughly every night before she crawled into her bed, which she made first thing every morning. All of her life, teachers had commented not on how brilliant she was or how creative or how clever, but on how "neat" her work was. It had seemed to impress them.

Neatness seemed to indicate to most people a sense of responsibility, as if keeping your appearance in order guaranteed that you could keep everything else in order, too. Meaning that you would be the perfect person to run fairs and carnivals and bazaars and committees and take care of all those tedious little details that messier people never wanted to bother with.

And the truth was, she *was* very good at that kind of thing. Hadn't had a flop yet.

But . . . she hated every minute of it. It wasn't who she was, not at all. If the people who always voted for her could have seen inside her mind, seen how tousled and tangled and chaotic it was, they'd have chosen someone else. If they could see how she had struggled with every assignment, every office, the organizing of every event, seen how she had to fight desperately for every moment of concentration, they might even have picked someone whose shirt trailed carelessly over the edge of a skirt or pair of jeans, someone whose clothes were always a mass of wrinkles and stains, someone whose hair was an untamed tangle of wild curls, as hers would be if it weren't for the ever-present barrettes.

Eve Forsythe was a fraud, but she was the only one who knew it. The person everyone saw . . . the neat, orderly, and organized Eve Elizabeth Forsythe, a dean's list freshman at Salem University, did exist. But only with great effort and concentration on the part of the *real* Eve Forsythe. The real Eve Elizabeth was a totally different human being. Dreamy. Vague. Unfocused, with thoughts and emotions as wild a jumble as any mass of thick, naturally curly hair. It was her mother, of course, who'd created the Eve Forsythe everyone saw.

When she was nine-and-a-half, her father had left the house, carrying only a suitcase and two boxes full of books. "Sorry, Kitten," he had said while her mother stood, stony-faced and silent, in the kitchen, "but this man's breaking out of jail, and the warden there," gesturing toward the kitchen, "says you can't come. Not fair to leave you here living under more rules and regulations than in any man's army, but I can't spring you." He knelt then to kiss her on the cheek. "I just hope you have the strength to escape one day. Don't wait too long, honey."

And he was gone, leaving her in the sole care of his soon-to-be-ex-wife, Nell Forsythe, who viewed the slightest speck of dust, the merest hint of disorder, and any unrestrained locks of curly hair with all the horror most people reserved for disasters like world wars, fatal plane crashes, and serial murders.

Eve had learned, very quickly, to pretend she hated those things, too. Because unlike her father, who was an adult, she *couldn't* leave. Not for a long, long time. As for fighting with her mother, what good would that do? If Richard Forsythe, a strong and strong-minded adult, hadn't had the strength to stand his ground and do battle against Nell, what chance did a shy, dreamy nine-year-old have? It was easier to give in and live the way her mother wanted.

Somewhere along the way, the myth that the daughter was as well organized, capable, and efficient as the mother had established itself, almost without Eve's awareness. And she had found herself heading one committee after another, organizing countless events, being elected to numerous offices.

Her mother was thrilled.

Eve wasn't stupid. She knew that the best way to dispel the myth was a simple one. All she had to do was screw up, big-time. All she had to do was ruin a major event. Forget an important detail, ignore a crucial phone call or note, miss repeated committee meetings. Not so difficult. Anyone can screw up, especially if they really want to.

But she couldn't do it. And it wasn't only Nell's wrath that she couldn't face. The thought of the disappointment and anger in the faces of her fellow students when the prom turned into a disaster or the fund-raising event was a failure or no one showed up for the concert, made her physically ill.

So she did it all, and she did it well. And everyone approved.

She had vowed that college would be different. True, she had agreed to study accounting instead of interior design the way she wanted, but that was only because Nell had laid down the law once again. It was accounting or nothing. "You have to earn a living," were the exact words. "Accounting is a good, solid profession. What is 'graphic arts,' anyway? Sounds like something that would appeal to your father. And look what happened to *him!*"

Eve's father had died two years earlier, unemployed and penniless. Which left Eve with no choices at all. It was accounting or nothing, so accounting it would be.

That was the first blow. The second was, although she had every intention when she left home of changing her image the very second she stepped onto the grounds of Salem University, she hadn't done it. At first, it was because she couldn't escape the clammy, uneasy feeling that her mother could somehow see her. By the time that feeling faded, it just seemed easier to brush her hair away from her face every morning and thrust its thickness into the clutches of the familiar barrettes. Easier, too, to wear the carefully matched sweaters and skirts her mother had picked out and then packed for her, easier to make her bed every morning and to color-coordinate her closet and alphabetize her CD's and use a Daytimer to keep her schedule straight. Easier, that's all.

Maybe later, when she had settled into her new routine, she would change her image. Maybe later . . .

But she had waited too long, and now here she was, cochair of the most important event of the year, the Founders' Day celebration jointly arranged by the university and the village of Twin Falls. The committee that she and Kevin cochaired was made up of five townspeople and five students. If the townspeople were chagrined at having young students on their committee, they handled their chagrin with grace and a spirit of cooperation.

That might well change, though, Eve thought, lifting her head to survey the traffic mess again, if this thing turns into a disaster. The whole town will blame us if something goes wrong.

She had done her best. It was harder, here at college. She hated accounting with a passion. It was boring and tedious and there was so much work. Finding the time for her committee duties was a struggle, and some nights she dragged into the dorm room so exhausted, she skipped flossing. Then she couldn't sleep, and had to struggle up out of bed and go into the bathroom and clean her teeth the way she'd been taught, just so she could sleep.

So much for changing her image.

What sickened her more than anything was knowing that if the Founders' Day celebration *did* go off perfectly, without a hitch, its success would condemn her to three more years of the same kind of life she'd always led. She'd be elected to more committees, more offices, she'd be called upon again and again to organize. She would be tagged throughout her entire college career with the label Andie had just applied to her: "The responsible, organized, capable, efficient Eve Forsythe."

Gag.

There were ten people on the committee. Two of the Twin Falls members, a nice, funny guy named Don and a small, heavy, blonde girl named Beth, were young. Eve had anticipated that one of them would be made chairperson.

She knew there were others on the committee who had actively sought the position, who wanted to sit in the chair at the head of the table, to be the "authority," the head, the person in power. Founders' Day was a very big deal, according to campus rumor. If all went well, there would be a certain amount of prestige for those who had pulled it all together. And if it didn't go off well?

Eve didn't want to think about that. Maybe

failing now *would* let her off the hook for future events. But the disgrace would be even worse here at college than it would have been in high school. Unbearable. And her mother would hear about it, maybe even yank her out of school.

She didn't want to be yanked out of school. Maybe she hadn't flowered on campus the way she'd hoped, but she loved it here. She didn't want to leave Salem, with its green, rolling lawns and its brick and stone buildings, its bell tower, the deep, wide river racing along behind the administration building. Most important, Nell Forsythe was three-hundred-and-eighty-seven miles away.

Spending the next three years chairing boring committees would be better than not being here at all. Better than being dragged back to the cold, sterile, atmosphere of the small frame house on Water Street in Doaks Landing, Pennsylvania.

The Founders' Day celebration had to be a success. It *had* to.

"Almost there," Andie announced, catapulting the car through an intersection just as the yellow light turned red. "Now all we need to do is find a place to park, which should be about as easy as straightening my hair."

She was right. Pennsylvania Avenue in

downtown Twin Falls was overflowing with parade spectators and every parking space for blocks was already taken. They had to park on Sixth Street, six blocks away, and dash down the side streets to find Kevin and the other members of the committee.

They found the group waiting in front of the post office, a huge red-brick building in the center of town.

"Everything's under control," Kevin assured Eve quickly when he saw how white and strained her face was. She could barely hear him over the noise of the crowd. "I know it looks like chaos, but the bands are lining up, the floats are in place, and the clowns are already tossing candy to keep the kids from rioting."

"It's not going to rain, is it?" she asked anxiously, glancing up at the charcoal-colored sky.

"Weatherman says no," Kevin answered firmly. He was tall and thin, neatly dressed in crisp chinos and a red Salem T-shirt, his light brown hair slightly windblown. Although he sounded confident, his eyes behind wire-rimmed glasses were as anxious as Eve's.

Eve liked Kevin. He had wanted this position more than she had, actively campaigning to be selected, and could have been annoyed that he had to share it with her. But he'd seemed to welcome her help. And he had been patient with her constant doubts and fears, assuring her that hiring a traveling carnival wouldn't be too expensive, that it would *not* rain, and that every horse in the campus equestrian club, the group holding last position in the long parade, would behave because they had all been in parades before. Quit worrying, Kevin told Eve.

They had worked hard. And they had worked well together, she thought.

Still . . . his eyes *did* reflect the same anxious expression she felt in her own.

"D day!" Serena Wolfe, a tall, blonde girl standing beside Kevin cried. She was thin and very pretty, wearing a chiffon, summery dress that fell to her ankles. Her blue eyes were wide with excitement and anticipation. Thin hands clutched Kevin's elbow, as if without that grip, she might find herself jumping up and down.

Serena's parents, Eve thought, had been way off base when they named their daughter. The girl was anything but serene. It was almost impossible to gauge her moods from one minute to the next. Sometimes she seemed quiet and relaxed, but more often she was bouncing around like a Ping-Pong ball, overflowing with nervous energy. But she had settled down and worked hard on the committee, and Eve was grateful.

"About time you got here," a voice said heavily in Eve's ear.

She groaned silently as she turned to face a short, good-looking boy so neatly dressed and groomed he always reminded Eve of a store-window mannequin. The only flaw on his perfect face was a small cut from shaving. His dark, straight hair was carefully slicked into place. He was the only guy in the group wearing a white shirt and tie.

"Hello, Alfred," she said coolly. "How's it going?" Not that she really wanted to know. Alfred had latched on to her at the very first committee meeting. She had known immediately that he wasn't someone she could ever be interested in, but Alfred wasn't easily discouraged. He called constantly, using the committee as an excuse, and often waited for her after the two classes they shared, math and parapsychology. Short of hitting him over the head with a brick, there didn't seem to be any way to get rid of Alfred.

He couldn't seem to grasp the concept of rejection.

"You're late," he accused, fixing his dark

eyes on her. "We've been waiting for hours. I thought you'd had an accident."

The thing Eve hated most about Alfred was his eyes — cold and hard, like little black marbles. Impossible to know what he was thinking.

Still, he, too, had worked hard on the Founders' Day celebration, even helping to set up the carnival, lifting heavy equipment, putting it in place until the early morning. Alfred wasn't very tall, but he was strong. His strength had proved very valuable.

Kevin glanced at his watch. "Well, it's time," he said heartily. "Let's get this show on the road. Literally."

So, after one last check to make sure the floats and the bands and the horses and the cars and rolling cannons and clowns were all present and in order, the whistle was blown and the parade celebrating the kickoff of the Founders' Day celebration began.

It was noisy and colorful, and things went as smoothly as Eve had hoped. The long parade marched from town to campus, the throng of spectators following along. Drums boomed, cymbals clanged, and horns tooted. Clowns armed with candy and cheap plastic whistles danced in and out of the crowd, entertaining them with foolish antics between parade units.

A traveling carnival hired by Eve had been set up in a huge field on the edge of Salem's campus. By the time the final unit arrived, the earlier units had already disbanded, with band members and float drivers and clowns still in costume milling about amid the game and food booths, and the rides. A huge, bright-yellow Ferris wheel hovered over the scene.

"We did it!" Eve breathed softly as the final horse from the equestrian club crossed the highway. "We actually did it! Everything went great, didn't it?"

She was standing in front of a large palomino horse ridden by a small, blonde girl named Alice. Eve knew her from parapsychology class. Alice was a friendly girl who loved to talk about her horse, Shadrack. She sat astride the horse as if she had been born in that position.

"Let's not get too close to these horses, okay?" Eve warned and, as if he'd heard her, the big palomino let out a sound that chilled the blood of those around it. Half-screech, half-neigh, a mixture of pain and fear and anger, it split the air like a siren. Before Alice could figure out what had happened or what to do about it, the horse reared up on its hind legs, still making that horrendous sound. When it landed, it began bucking wildly, snorting furiously.

Eve watched with horrified eyes as Alice struggled to regain control, her knuckles white on the reins.

But it was hopeless. The horse was completely out of control.

Alice lost the battle. Eve and the others stood frozen in shock as the small figure was tossed out of the saddle and into the air as if she weighed no more than a feather. She crashed to the ground at Eve's feet. Her body hit the earth with a soft but deadly smacking sound. Her head flopped lifelessly. A second after she landed, blood began pouring out from beneath her black velvet riding helmet, staining the bright green grass around her.

People ran toward the horse in an effort to stop its wild bucking and spinning in circles. But they quickly backed away at the sight of the deadly, flying hooves.

The animal, still bucking frantically, ducked its head, snorted in rage, and galloped toward the crowd of spectators in the distance, milling about beneath the big yellow Ferris wheel.

Chapter 2

Bucking and spinning, its deadly hooves lashing out repeatedly, Alice's palomino lurched toward the crowds gathered beneath the lemon yellow Ferris wheel and standing in front of the bright red game and refreshment booths. The band members still in uniform, the costumed clowns, and the spectators who had marched from town were all anxious for the refreshment booths to open. They needed to quench their thirst after the long walk. Continuing to talk and laugh among themselves, they failed to hear the shouts of alarm behind them.

While a panicked Kevin and Eve ran alongside the horse, Serena and Andie ran to Alice's side and knelt on the ground. Serena used the hem of her long dress in an attempt to stop the flow of blood pouring from the head wound.

Alfred hung back, insisting, "I don't know anything about horses!"

Two men from town ran toward the animal. They quickly backed away again when they saw that attempting to grab the reins would be sheer folly, if not suicidal. The rest of the spectators who had trailed onto campus along with the equestrian club continued to retreat, watching in frozen silence.

"Do something!" Eve screamed at Kevin as they ran along beside the frenzied animal, ducking to avoid the wicked hooves. "We have to stop him!"

Kevin tried, lunging in underneath the horse's head, his hand outstretched to grab the reins. He was careful, darting in and out of the path of the palomino's frantic bucking.

He never got close enough to grab the leather straps. On his third desperate attempt, the horse swung around abruptly. His left hind hoof came out in a wicked slash and caught Kevin directly in the midsection, lifting him up off his feet and flinging him backward. Kevin let out only a small, startled sound as he went up and out and then down, slamming into the ground with the wind knocked out of him and several ribs painfully shattered. He lay on the grass stunned, his face twisted in agony, his eyes blank with shock.

"Kevin!" Eve screamed again, her cheekbones white with terror. But when she tried to run to his aid, the horse lurched between them, bucking and snorting. Then it raced away, toward the crowd.

Shouting at the people behind her to help Kevin, Eve ran after the horse.

Stopping it was out of the question. All she could do was scream a warning.

Too late. More screams rang out as the crazed horse lunged into the crowd. People began racing for their lives, in their panic stumbling over one another, pushing, shoving. Some tripped and fell, others stumbled over the fallen, and lay there, too stunned to move.

It seemed to Eve, watching with horrified eyes, that there were bodies everywhere. The noise level was horrendous, with screams and sobs and shouts of fear mixing with the horse's furious snorting. The sounds tore at her ears. She wanted them to stop, but she didn't know how to make that happen.

She saw the clown out of the corner of her eye. He was tall, broad-shouldered in his pink and yellow and turquoise polka-dotted suit, a matching tall, coned hat sitting on his head, thick white makeup on his face. He had a huge, bright red mouth, and fat teardrops had been painted on his cheeks with a black makeup crayon. He approached the horse cautiously, one hand in an oversized white glove outstretched, whispering softly as he moved closer to the bucking animal.

"It's okay, it's okay," he kept repeating quietly as he lifted giant, floppy black shoes carefully, taking one tentative step and then another and another.

The horse continued to buck, but its ears stood up.

"It's okay, boy," the clown murmured, "just take it easy, take it easy, it's okay."

The murmuring had its effect on the crowd. The screaming stopped, people halted in their frantic flight, and a sudden hush fell over the area.

Eve held her breath.

"There, there, it's okay, we'll fix it," the clown said, so close to the horse now that Eve could almost feel its hot breath melting the white makeup. "Whatever it is, we'll fix it, I promise. Calm down now, just calm down."

The horse stopped bucking.

The oversized white glove reached out and gently took the reins, while the other gloved hand began stroking the palomino's pale mane. Although the horse trembled, it made no attempt to escape the hand.

A sigh of relief rippled through the on-lookers.

After a moment, the clown moved easily, quietly to the side, one hand firmly grasping the reins. The other hand moved cautiously to the saddle and began a gentle search.

"Here it is," a deep voice said matter-of-factly, pulling something from beneath the saddle and holding it high in the air for all to see. "I knew there had to be something. No wonder the poor thing went nuts. Wouldn't we all if we had something like this digging into our skin?"

Shaking with both relief and shock, Eve moved closer. The fat white glove was holding within its folds a . . . burr. A nasty, prickly, burr with dozens of sharp edges. There were tons of them along the highway, all as painful as a porcupine's quills if they came into contact with human flesh. Or animal flesh.

"That was under his saddle?" she asked the clown.

He nodded. "Under the saddle blanket. Digging right into his skin," he said.

"How did you know that's what it was?"

"I didn't. But I knew it had to be something. It was either that or locoweed and," he laughed, "I don't think you have much of that around here."

"You know a lot about horses," Eve said admiringly, her voice husky with relief. "You just saved a whole lot of lives."

"Raised in Texas," he said as two men from the carnival arrived to lead the exhausted horse away. "But I live in Twin Falls now. You know the camera shop in town. Draper's?"

Eve knew it. A neat, trim, small white house on Pennsylvania Avenue. She had had film developed there. But the only two people in the shop had been an older man with thick white hair and . . . a tall, good-looking dark-haired boy in a blue T-shirt. She had dealt only with the older man. Impossible to match that good-looking boy with this white-painted face, over-sized red mouth, and astonished crayoned eyebrows.

The ambulances arrived, sirens screeching. The shrill sound snapped Eve back to the present, shuddering as she remembered Kevin and Alice. Forgetting the clown, she turned and ran back to where the two were being lifted onto stretchers.

Kevin was still conscious, although his face was ashen with pain.

"You'll be okay," Eve said as he was being loaded into the ambulance. She tried to smile. "You have to be okay, Kevin. I can't do this all by myself. If you desert me on the very first day of this thing, I'll never forgive you."

Then the doors closed. Eve felt totally alone.

But she wasn't. "You're assuming this celebration will continue?" Alfred's voice said from behind her.

Eve turned to glare at him with disgust. He hadn't helped at all, not one little bit. He still looked as neat and perfect as he had earlier. Not a hair out of place.

Serena, white-faced, her flowered dress stained with Alice's blood, was right behind him. Andie stood beside her. "You think the administration will cancel because of what just happened?" Eve asked them.

Serena shook her head. While she was tending Alice, she had pushed a strand or two of her long, pale hair away from her face. Those strands were streaked now with thick, dark red. Alice's blood. "Who knows? So many people were hurt. Alice has had that horse forever. What made him go nuts like that?"

Eve explained. She told them about the clown taming the panicked horse.

"Poor horse," Serena commented, but Alfred scolded, "Reserve your sympathy for the people on their way to the hospital. I'm just grateful I'm not one of them."

"How could you possibly be?" Eve asked sharply. "You got out of the way so fast."

Alfred winced. "You're not mad, are you? I

mean, like I said, I don't know the first thing about horses. I was afraid if I did the wrong thing, I'd make everything worse, that's all."

Sure, Eve thought. Aloud, she said, "Is Alice going to be okay? " and knew immediately by the look on Serena's face that Alice was not going to be okay.

"She wasn't breathing," Serena said. "And there was so much blood . . ."

Eve felt sick.

"But maybe the ambulance attendants can do something," Serena added hastily. "What about the people over there, where you were?" She pointed toward the Ferris wheel. "Was anyone . . . killed?"

Eve swallowed. "I don't think so." She remembered then that she hadn't even thanked the clown who had quieted the horse. "I have to go back and see if I can find that guy. The one who found the burr. Come with me? And we'd better get the committee together to see what needs to be done. Maybe you're right, Alfred," she added as they began to walk. "Maybe the whole celebration will be canceled now. Maybe it *should* be. Burr or not, that horse going crazy and hurting people could be an omen. A *bad* omen."

Alfred grunted. "Since when are *you* superstitious? I distinctly remember you saying in parapsychology class that you didn't believe in anything paranormal. You said you thought ESP and telekinesis, stuff that Dr. Litton talks about in class, were nonsense. You said if anyone *our* age had special powers, there'd be no such things as SAT's. Everybody laughed."

"And a lot of people in class agreed with me," Eve pointed out. "I'm not the only one who thinks all that stuff is stupid and silly. A lot of people in that class are only taking it for extra credit, like me. Kevin was making jokes about paranormal stuff, and so was Alice." She fell silent, thinking of Alice slamming into the ground. "When I said omen, I just meant that it's not a good sign when disaster strikes on the very first day of an event."

As they walked toward the Ferris wheel, Eve saw no sign of the clown who had calmed the horse. Maybe he'd decided this wasn't a safe place to be, and had already gone back to town. She couldn't blame him. And judging from the way the crowd had thinned, he wasn't the only one.

Her heart sank. The goal was to make money for the new science building. How could they make any money if people were scared away on the very first day? And what if Kevin wasn't able to return and help her? True, she still had the rest of the committee. But she and Kevin had been working so well together. She needed his quiet reassurance.

Then again, if the whole event was canceled, she wouldn't have to worry about it anymore. And it wouldn't even be her fault. *She* hadn't put that burr under the horse's saddle.

Strange thought. Of course she hadn't. But maybe that was worth thinking about. "How would a burr get under a saddle?" she mused aloud, her eyes scanning the sparse crowd for some sign of the white-faced clown. "I mean, I know there are tons of burrs along the highway, but one wouldn't jump up and implant itself under a saddle, would it?"

Alfred stopped walking and turned to look at her. "What does *that* mean? Are you hinting that someone put that burr there on purpose?"

Serena, too, stared at Eve. "Eve, why would someone do that? And wouldn't he have been seen? I mean, there were people walking along with the equestrian club the whole time."

"Alice stopped a couple of times, remember?" Eve reminded them. "She was having a problem with her boot or her stirrup or something. None of us stayed behind with her. We kept marching. She caught up with us a few minutes later."

Alfred rubbed his chin. "And you think someone could have sneaked up behind her then and stuck that burr under her saddle? With her *sitting* in it?"

Eve shook her head. "I don't know. I know it sounds stupid, and I can't imagine why anyone would want to do something so cruel. But it's hard to believe a burr would have lodged itself under the saddle without some help."

"Could have been blown by the wind," Serena said. "It's very windy, Eve, has been all day. Look at the trees along campus, they're bending almost double."

That was true enough. And the round, prickly burrs didn't weigh much. Was it possible that one of them had been yanked off its bush by a vigorous wind and implanted under Alice's saddle?

It had to be possible. Because the idea that someone would have deliberately done it was too ridiculous to even consider.

Unable to locate the clown who had quieted the horse, Eve gave up the search. She knew where the guy worked. She could always go into town later and thank him.

The important thing now was to call an emergency meeting of the committee and head on over to the administration building to see if the celebration was being canceled.

It wasn't.

When the cause of the incident had been explained to the dean, she said thoughtfully, "This event has been planned for some time. You've all worked very hard on it, and its success is important to the university. In spite of this very unfortunate accident, I believe the celebration must go on."

There were nods of approval all around. Eve's head didn't move.

"I have spoken with one of the doctors at the hospital in town," the dean continued. Her expression suddenly became very bleak. "There was nothing they could do for Alice. That is tragic. But canceling the planned events will not bring her back. I have also spoken with her parents. Although they are distraught, they have assured me that Alice herself would have wanted the celebration to continue. Therefore, I have decided that we will dedicate the entire week to her memory, and use a portion of the carnival funds to establish a scholarship fund in her name. I believe her parents would like that."

Still Eve said nothing. Her eyes were focused on a large, round clock on the wall behind the dean's desk. Only two o'clock in the afternoon. The parade had begun at noon. Shouldn't it be later than it was? Shouldn't it be, like, *days* later? If it were, for instance, next Sunday now, the whole Founders' Day event would be behind her. She could lie on her bed in her room and relax, knowing that she had nothing more important to do that day than call her mother, as she always did on Sunday.

But it *wasn't* next Sunday. It was *this* Sunday. Only the first day of the festivities. Hard to believe now, that her biggest concern last night when she finally fell asleep had been that it might rain, ruining the parade. It hadn't rained on her parade. What had happened was worse. Much worse.

"By the way," the dean added, "I have some good news. Kevin's injuries are painful, but not that serious. He'll be back to help you and the committee by Tuesday, Wednesday at the latest. That should cheer you up some."

It helped a little, knowing that Kevin would be back later in the week. But it didn't help a lot. Eve still felt as if a heavy black cloak had draped itself over her shoulders. Because something she had never once thought to write down on her List of Possible Problems, had happened.

Someone had died.

It was only the first day of the celebration, and someone had died.

And there were still six-and-a-half days to go.

Chapter 3

The Founders' Day committee returned silently to the carnival site. All were visibly shaken.

Eve glanced around her, struggling to organize her thoughts. The debris left by the horse's rampage had disappeared, and the scene seemed very normal. The sunflower-yellow Ferris wheel was revolving swiftly now. It was only half-full. Screams of fear and excitement echoed from the precariously swaying seats as they reached the very top, high above the campus. More shrieks came from wilder rides such as Devil's Elbow, Hell on Wheels, Space Demon, and The Snake. People were buying popcorn and cotton candy and hot dogs and cold drinks, while others moved from the dart booth to the shooting gallery and bottle toss booths, seeking to win a giant panda bear or a small portable tape player. Balloons in vivid colors trailed along behind small children. There were already half a dozen of the round globes floating up into the sky, and more would join them soon enough as additional strings escaped small hands.

There were shocked eyes in some faces, muted whispers of horrors from others, but it seemed clear to Eve that those who had been affected most severely by the disaster had left campus, leaving behind those who were dismayed but determined not to let anything ruin their day. There was now a good-sized crowd, and newcomers were visible arriving at the entrance to campus.

The Founders' Day celebration would continue.

The scene in front of Eve looked like an ordinary carnival site on an ordinary Sunday afternoon.

But what she was seeing instead was blood pooling under Alice's broken body. Instead of the music and the laughter, she heard again the sharp snap of Kevin's ribs cracking.

Eve knew she would hear and see those things for a long time.

It shouldn't *look* normal, Eve thought, moving toward the cotton candy booth to make sure all was in order. How can everything look so ordinary when someone died just a little while ago?

Suppose she'd been right about Alice's death being a bad omen? Suppose it was only the beginning . . . ?

Stop that! she commanded herself sharply. Stop it right now. It *wasn't* an omen. There's no such thing as an omen. You're being silly and stupid. The best way to put what's happened out of your mind, at least for now, is to keep busy. And with Kevin in the infirmary, there's plenty to do. So get to it, girl!

It wasn't easy. Shock and sadness weighed her down. Every step she took, every movement she made, was an effort at first. But after a while, it became automatic, as exercising her responsibilities always did.

Alfred wouldn't leave her side, repeatedly asking her anxiously if she was mad at him because he hadn't helped with the horse.

Telling him, "No, Alfred, if I were mad, I'd *say* so," she sent him on an errand and went into the cotton candy booth. She had just dipped a finger into one of the huge sacks of sugar piled against the back wall and was tasting it when an amused voice from the other side of the counter said, "Eating up all the profits? That's not fiscally sound."

Flushing, Eve looked up into dark brown eyes that seemed to be laughing at her. She stood up very straight. "I was just checking to make sure they sent us the right thing," she said stiffly. "Besides, I didn't realize someone was spying on me!"

The boy was tall and good-looking. Not gorgeous. But nice cheekbones and very intelligent eyes. Thick, dark, curly hair, slightly damp across his forehead. His white T-shirt bore the words, DRAPER'S CAMERA SHOP, TWIN FALLS. Underneath that, in smaller letters, Eve read, *Come In and See What Develops.*

This was the guy she'd seen at Draper's. Which meant, he was the clown who had tamed Alice's horse.

The sharpness of her remark erased the laughter from his eyes. "I just wanted to see how that girl was," he said, using the same brusque tone of voice she'd used. "The one thrown by the horse."

It was him, all right. He looked very different in his T-shirt and cutoffs, his face free of the thick white makeup, but she would have known that voice anywhere. Even if the tone he'd just used was very different from the soothing voice that had quieted Shadrack.

Chagrin washed over her. He had saved a

lot of people and not even waited to be thanked, and now she'd been rude to him.

She came out of the booth quickly, saying, "I'm sorry. I'm really sorry. I didn't recognize you, but I'm glad you came back. No one got a chance to thank you. I'm Eve Forsythe. And I thank you."

His eyes thawed again, and he smiled. "No problem. You mean I should have hung around, maybe got my picture in the local paper?" He gestured toward the camera slung over his shoulder. "Couldn't happen. The paper's photographer was otherwise occupied at the time. Had some crazed horseflesh on his hands."

"You? You take pictures for the newspaper in Twin Falls?" He looked awfully young to be a professional news photographer.

"Right. Garth Draper. My dad owns the local camera shop. I run it part-time, and work for the paper as a sideline. I mean," he added, shrugging, "it's not like a heck of a lot goes on in Twin Falls that requires a full-time newspaper photographer." His expression sobered quickly. "Not counting today, of course."

"Did you take pictures?" Eve asked quickly, picturing the earlier, horrifying scene splashed across the front page of the Twin Falls Gazette. No one who saw it would come anywhere near the carnival.

But he shook his head. "I took a few of the general scene, and there *will* be a story. I saw our ace reporter, Maxine Tremblay, jotting down notes. But there won't be any pictures of the girl or the other people who were hurt. No shattered bodies, no bloodied flesh. I'm not into that stuff."

Eve breathed a sigh of relief. Still, the article would be bad publicity for the Founders' Day celebration. Would they be able to overcome it?

They *had* to. Not just because she couldn't stand the thought of screwing up. There was that scholarship in Alice's name. That was important.

"So, how is she? That girl?" Garth asked as they began to move away from the steadily increasing crowd at the cotton candy booth.

"Oh. She . . . she didn't make it. She had a severe head injury. Serena and the others tried to help, but it was too late." Too late . . .

He paled. "Geez, I'm sorry. Was she a friend of yours?"

"I knew her. She was in my parapsychology class." Eve hesitated, then added, "It's not that she was a really good friend of mine or anything. But she was nice. And I've never seen anything like that before. I still can't believe it. And then," she spread her hands to include the scene around her, "to see everything going on as if nothing happened, well, it just seems too weird, that's all." She leaned against the Ferris wheel's ticket booth and looked up at him. "The thing is, I'm sort of in charge, me and the committee, and I'd have canceled it if I'd had my way. But the dean and Alice's parents thought the celebration should go on, so here we are."

"I can see how you'd feel," he said, nodding. "But canceling all of this . . ." he glanced around as Eve had done earlier . . . "would be no small feat. And it really wouldn't do that girl any good, would it?"

"No." Eve felt depression sliding over her. If only the sun would come out. But it was almost evening now, and the sky hadn't brightened. It looked more like rain now than it had before. Another bad omen?

To change the subject, she said, "Do you go to Salem?"

"Did go. Two years. But last spring the dean and I came to an understanding. We both agreed it would be mutually satisfying for both parties if I brought my matriculation to a speedy conclusion."

"You were kicked out?"

There was such horror in Eve's voice, that Garth laughed. "Not exactly. We . . . the photography department, that is, were putting on a photo exhibit. Contemporary photographers, starring some of my idols. We had it all set up, and all of a sudden, out of nowhere, comes this uptight alum who threw a fit over the nudes. "And this alum donates many, many big bucks to Salem University. I went to the dean. She wrestled with the problem, and took my side. Said the nudes would stay. She's okay, the dean."

"If the dean agreed with you, why were you thrown out?"

"I told you, I wasn't thrown out. The dean said the photos stayed, so the alum went to the board of trustees. The board wasn't about to cut off that kind of heavy-duty funding. The photos came down. Nothing the dean could do. But I was pissed. I got together a ragtag band of protestors and we blocked the entrance to the art building. I said we wouldn't move until the photos went back up. The board said they weren't going back up. So Don Quixote here pulled this stupid grandstand play and shouted, for the whole campus to hear, that either the photos went back up or I left." He laughed without rancor. "I left. A few credits short of my associate degree in photography."

"I'm sorry," Eve said. She didn't know what else to say.

He shrugged. "Don't be. I figured, anything Salem hadn't taught me about photography, my dad could teach me. I was right. Before he retired and bought the camera shop, he was a pro. Worked for the best regional magazine in Texas. Anything he doesn't know about taking pictures probably isn't worth knowing."

Serena, Andie, and Alfred arrived to tell Eve that everything seemed to be "going okay" and to comment on the size of the crowd. "I know it's weird," Andie said, "but it looks like we'll do okay tonight. Amazing! I thought when word spread through town about that horse going crazy, no one would show up."

Alfred nodded. "Me, too. I guess people figure it was a freak thing that couldn't possibly happen twice, and aren't worried. That's nice for us, I guess."

Eve said nothing. No matter how successful the Founders' Day celebration was, Alice would still be dead.

Andie looked up at the sky. "I wish it weren't so cloudy. The carnival might look more interesting under a full moon."

"Weird things happen when there's a full

moon," Alfred said sullenly. His eyes, too, were surveying Garth, but with more resentment than interest. "Suicides, murders, you hear about them all the time on the news when the moon is full."

"Alfred, you're as superstitious as I am," Serena said. "Funny. You don't look like the type. You look so . . . so *practical*."

Alfred must have considered that a compliment, because he smiled.

"Alfred's right, though," Andie said after Eve had introduced Garth. "I've heard that a full moon makes people do weird things. It has something to do with the tides."

"There's no ocean in Twin Falls, Andie," Eve said dryly. They weren't going to start discussing paranormal junk again, were they?

"Doesn't have to be," Andie replied. "The whole phenomenon of the full moon's effect is planetary, not regional. We're *all* affected by it. Ask Dr. Litton."

Dr. Litton was their parapsychology professor. Eve found her fun and interesting, even though most of the stuff she talked about was totally off the wall.

Alfred declared starvation, as he frequently did, and Eve was grateful when Serena and Andie dragged him off to the hot dog booth, leaving her alone with Garth. That was fine with her.

"That guy's really hung up on you," Garth commented when the trio was out of hearing. "Can't blame him, even if you do wear your hair like my sixth-grade teacher."

Eve's left hand instinctively flew to her barrette. "What's wrong with my hair?" she said testily.

"Nothing wrong with it. It's great hair. So why are you holding it prisoner? Makes you look uptight and nervous. My sixth-grade teacher was very uptight."

"Maybe I *am* uptight and nervous!" she snapped. "It's been a crummy day, in case you've forgotten. And why did you pick *me* to ask about Alice, anyway? Why didn't you just ask someone else?"

"Because you were the girl who was running after the horse when I stopped it. So I figured you'd know what had happened to its rider."

Startled, Eve looked up, one hand still self-consciously fingering her barrette. He had remembered her? Out of all that confusion and chaos, he had remembered what she looked like? That pleasing thought was quickly followed by the fact that he had remembered her as looking "nervous and uptight."

Well, she *was* nervous. Who wouldn't be? Why wasn't *everyone?*

"By the way," he added quickly, "I really liked my sixth-grade teacher. It was her first year of teaching, and she *was* uptight. But she was also the prettiest woman in the building."

Eve smiled.

"So," he said, relaxing, "do you have any major duties that you have to take care of right now?"

"No. I don't think so. Everything's okay, I guess, if you can call it that after what happened." Distant thunder sounded just then, and a streak of silver lightning lit up the purpled, twilight sky. Eve groaned. "I really don't want it to rain. If it'll just hold off until ten o'clock, I swear I'll never complain about rain again as long as I live."

"Sure, you will. But since standing out here watching the sky for bad weather doesn't sound like a whole lot of fun, let's go check out the Mirror Maze."

Eve smiled again. "Sure. I watched them set the whole thing up yesterday. Looked very confusing to me. Might be just what I need to take my mind off . . . everything. As long as we don't get lost in there."

"We won't get lost. I was an Eagle Scout.

Could find my way out of anything, with or without a compass." He took her hand. "Let's go exploring."

Another bolt of lightning lit up the sky as Garth led Eve toward the Mirror Maze, and the thunderclap that followed sounded ominously close.

Chapter 4

I know you're up there, Moon, even though you're hiding. It doesn't matter how many clouds are in the night sky, I can always feel your presence. And you're watching, aren't you? Watching to see what happens, watching to see when and how I'll need you.

Well, I will need you, and very soon. I didn't need your help today. That was something anyone could have done. Simple. Requiring no more power than a sneaky little movement on my part. No one was paying any attention.

And I can do other things on my own. Little things.

But when it comes to the big stuff, I'll have to use the power, and I expect you to help, like you always do. They all think it's a coincidence that there's a full moon just as the celebration begins. But it's not. I planned it that way. I knew I'd need your help, so I used the power to make sure the dates chosen were the right ones.

And now I need to save up all my energy for the really important things.

But you will help, won't you? Like you always do? I know that much of my power comes from you. I don't know how or why that's so, but I know that it is. If the celebration had taken place when you were just a tiny little sliver of silver, I don't know what I would have done. Everything would have been ruined.

They laugh at us, you know. They make jokes about any kind of special power. They say there is no such thing. Not Doctor Litton, though. She believes. I can tell. But the rest of them don't. Their crude jokes make me sick! Sick and furious! How dare they? How dare they ridicule something just because they haven't experienced it?

They will now, though, won't they? They will definitely experience the power. By the time this week is over, all of them will realize that you don't have to understand something to believe in it. They'll know there are things in this world that can't be explained.

Alice knows that now. She checked that horse's coat thoroughly before she tossed that saddle blanket over his pale, shiny back, didn't she? There were no burrs anywhere in sight.

If there had been, she would have lovingly, carefully removed them. When that horse she trusted so much threw her, her last thought must have been, I don't understand. So she died knowing, as the other do not, that there are many, many things in this world that make no sense.

They need to learn that. They need to stop their ridicule, their crude jokes, their stupid, careless contempt for the paranormal. Fools!

And with your help, oh, shiny, silver Moon, I can see to it that they do stop. Together, we can see to it that they learn their lesson.

Especially her. She's the worst. She says that ESP and telekinesis and all special powers are phony, but she's the real phony. She thinks I don't know it, but I do. She's scared to death that this whole week is going to be a big disaster and that everyone will blame her. I can see it in her eyes.

All I have to do is make sure that when that happens, exactly as she feared, she'll understand that it really had nothing to do with her. That I was the one who wrecked it all. Me. All by myself.

Well, not exactly all by myself. I do need your help.

And I know you'll come through for me.

All that screaming today, all those people

flying through the air, the sound of bones snapping like breadsticks, wasn't that exciting? Lovely sounds, just lovely. Well worth the wait.

And more of the same on the way.

All the joking, all the laughter, will turn on them. And guess who's going to have the last laugh?

Me.

When I was little, my mother used to say that my father was so proud of me, he acted like I'd hung the Moon.

Was he right? Is that why you're always on my side?

I can still hear all that screaming ringing in my ears.

What a lovely sound.

I can hardly wait to hear it again.

Chapter 5

The Mirror Maze was a squat, windowless building that had been set up at the rear of the carnival site, a safe distance away from the loud music and shrill screams of the other rides. There was no line at the ticket booth, and no one seemed to be going into or coming out of the box-shaped structure with three narrow wooden steps leading up to the entrance. A painted sign over the door read, AMAZING MIRROR MAZE! YOU MAY NEVER COME OUT!

The girl sitting on a stool in the booth was attempting to read a textbook. Her eyes were half-closed with boredom. "Hasn't been busy at all," she told them as she handed them their tickets. "The maze is pretty tame stuff compared to the Devil's Elbow and Hell on Wheels and The Snake." She made a face of displeasure. "I thought I'd get some homework done, but I also thought I'd see at least a few friendly faces. I've had more fun sound asleep."

Eve smiled. "Remember, it's for a good cause."

The girl quirked an eyebrow at her. "You *would* say something like that," and returned to her book.

Eve flushed, wishing Garth hadn't heard that remark. It made her sound so . . . so pompous or self-righteous or something. But the really scary thing was, it was exactly the kind of thing her mother often said.

Nell Forsythe had never remarried, filling her life instead with charity committees, things she liked to call "good works." Eve had been enlisted to help more than once, and whenever anyone, including Eve, complained about the long hours or the hard work, Nell would tighten her lips and say, "Remember, it's for a good cause."

I sounded exactly like her a minute ago, Eve thought, shuddering. Everyone said that girls always turned into their mothers. It was a fear that haunted Eve every day of her life. Was it already happening? So soon?

"Scared?" Garth said, seeing her shudder. "It's not a haunted house, Eve, it's just a maze of mirrors."

"No," she said quickly, "why would I be

scared?" She wasn't about to confess to him what she was really afraid of. She hardly knew him. "But I wish there were more people here. It's awfully quiet."

And indeed, once they were inside the low-ceilinged building, the quiet deepened. The place was well lit so that people could make their way through the intricate maze. But every footstep on the scuffed floor echoed like tom-toms. Although it was still warm outside, inside it seemed damp and chilly to Eve. Suddenly, her plaid cotton blouse wasn't nearly warm enough. She had to hug her arms around her chest to keep from shivering.

"You *are* scared," Garth said, stopping at the entrance to the maze to look down at her with concerned eyes. "We don't have to go in here, Eve. We can find something else to do."

"I'm not scared," she repeated. "I'm just cold. No wonder people are steering clear of this place. You could store fresh meat in here and it wouldn't spoil."

Garth laughed. "It's not that cold. Good for the circulation. So, you ready or what?"

"Ready." At least the place wasn't dark. It would be stupid to fill a place with mirrors and then make it too dark for anyone to see their reflection. Still, the place *felt* dark. Maybe because it was so cold and quiet. "We *are* staying together, right?"

"Of course."

The mirrors lining the maze's passageways were ordinary mirrors, not the curvy, wavy ones found in funhouses at amusement parks. The long, narrow glass sections were lined up along the walls like soldiers marching down a field. Only the ceiling and floor were wood.

Garth was disappointed. "Well, this is a bust," he said as they slowly wound their way from one passageway into another, constantly facing their own reflections.

"It's not that I don't enjoy looking at your reflection, because I do, but I'm already sick of my own face staring back at me. There have to be a lot more interesting things to do at a carnival than see myself multiplied before my very eyes. One of me is more than enough. Come on, let's get out of here."

Eve agreed, and decided that the Mirror Maze wasn't going to be bringing in big bucks. Maybe they'd make it up on the other rides.

But getting out of the maze proved to be easier said than done.

"This is ridiculous!" Garth said when they had retraced their steps three times. Each time, instead of arriving at the exit, they found themselves facing twelve more mirror images of themselves. Ten mirror sections lined each side of the wall, with each glass panel repeating the image in the panel beside it. The two double end panels did the same. There were twenty-four Garths and twenty-four Eves staring back at them, and all twenty-four faces looked annoyed.

There was no evidence of an exit anywhere near them.

"I was sure we came in this way," Eve murmured, "weren't you?"

Garth nodded grimly. "Okay, let's try turning left," he said, moving ahead of her. "Not that we have much choice. The exit's gotta be in this direction."

But it wasn't. They encountered only another dead end.

"I'll go first this time," Eve said, turning around. She could feel her nerves beginning to fray. She was beginning to hate the sight of all those Eves and Garths, and she wanted *out*.

"Ouch," Garth said from behind her when she took the lead. "Do you have any idea how humiliating it is for a former Eagle Scout to let someone else go first in a search?"

But Eve knew he was following as, stepping up the pace, she wove steadily in and out of the narrow corridors, her hands feeling the walls, her eyes searching, for a way out. And she believed that he was still behind her when she reached yet another dead end and, sighing in exasperation, turned to face him.

He wasn't there.

There was only, at the far end of the corridor, the shiny reflection of a tall, slender girl in a plaid blouse and navy blue skirt, her dark hair pulled severely away from a face that looked very pale. Her eyes seemed huge, as if the glass was magnifying them.

"Garth?" Her voice echoed eerily in the midst of all that quiet. "Garth?"

No answer.

Eve took a few uncertain steps forward. "Garth? Where are you?"

The only sound she heard was a sharp, angry thunderclap overhead, followed by a brutal gust of wind that rattled the building's none-too-solid boards and made the glass panels shake.

It's probably raining, too, Eve thought bitterly, although there was no rat-a-tat-tat sound on the roof. When I get out of here, it'll be pouring and I'll walk out into a sea of mud. Everyone will have gone home, like rats deserting a sinking ship.

When I get out of here quickly changed to *if* I get out of here. Suddenly apprehensive, she whirled to retrace her steps again.

She had just turned yet another corner when a voice that seemed to come out of nowhere said softly, *"Eve. That's not the way out."*

Eve stopped in her tracks. "Garth? Is that you?"

"Eve," the voice said again, so faintly Eve could barely hear it, *"you're going the wrong way. But then, it really doesn't matter, does it?"*

Glancing around for any sign of another human being and finding nothing but her own reflection staring back at her, Eve pressed her back against the mirrored wall. The glass felt cold. "Who's there? Who is that?"

"It doesn't matter that you're going the wrong way." The words were soft, as if encased in silk. *"Because you're never going to get out of here."* A low giggle. *"Not alive, anyway."*

Eve's jaw dropped. The lights overhead, bouncing off the mirrored walls, hurt her eyes. "What . . . what are you talking about? Where *are* you?"

"Oh, Eve," in a regretful, almost sad voice, *"don't get upset. I hate to see you wasting your energy looking for a way out. There isn't one. Not for you."*

Eve's head swung from side to side, her eyes searching, seeking, finding nothing, no physical form to attach to the disembodied whisper, nothing to reveal the location of her tormentor. She was still very much alone in the corridor, but twenty-four images of herself stared back at her as if to say, *You'll get no help from us.* "This isn't funny!" she cried. "What do you want? Why can't you tell me the way out?"

The voice, although still low and hard to hear, sharpened slightly. *"I told you, there isn't one. Not for you, Eve. Not ever."*

Suddenly, there was a sharp cracking sound and the end mirror on the wall opposite Eve, the one farthest from her, exploded in a shower of glass.

Eve gasped, one hand flying up to cover her mouth.

A second later, the mirror next to the first one exploded, then the third one, as if an invisible vandal were marching up the aisle toward Eve, tossing large, heavy objects into the glass panels opposite her. The worn, wooden floor was already littered with large and small fragments of glass, and where the mirrors had been only seconds before, gray-brown boards stared out at Eve.

Eve's eyes took in the mess with horror. Navigating through it in her black flats would be dangerous.

A fourth mirror, no more than a few feet

from Eve, shattered. A thick shard of glass narrowly missed her left arm.

There were only six mirrors left on that side of the wall. The last one was directly opposite Eve.

"Oh, God," she whispered, and turned and ran, in the only direction open to her. She ran straight toward the carpet of glass.

Behind her, the voice called softly, *"Oh, didn't I make myself clear? Running from me is a total waste of time."*

Chapter 6

Look at her run! Feet in those flimsy little shoes flying over the broken glass. Should have worn sneakers, the little twit. Glass'll slice right through those thin soles easy as slicing cheese. So proper, so perfect, so responsible, but too dumb to wear sneakers in a place full of glass.

Okay, so it wasn't full of glass when she came in. But anything can happen in a house full of mirrors, right? Someone could have been watching when they put this building up and someone could then find a way into the passageways behind the panels and smack the mirrors good and hard from the back with, say, a big, fat hammer, so the glass explodes all over the place. That could happen.

She should have known that could happen. Always making lists, I've seen her. Should *have put this on her list of Things That Can Happen.*

Well, she knows it now.

Too late.

There she goes, running again. Yelling for help at the top of her lungs. Lot of good that'll do her. I'm certainly not helping her. Why should I?

She took from me the best chance I had to show off my power to everyone. If I were heading this committee, the way I should have been, the way I would be if things were fair, I could have used my power to make this the best, most amazing celebration ever held anywhere. I could have done things that never could have been explained logically. Maybe I would have used my power to put on a giant fireworks display in the sky, just let them explode up there whenever I felt like it, without anything set up on the ground. No one would be able to explain that, that's for sure, not even Miss Logical, Analytical Genius.

Fireworks would have popped everyone's eyes, wouldn't they? I know I could have pulled it off, especially with Moon out in full force, feeding my power.

Another scream . . . If she keeps making all that racket, someone could hear her, even over the carnival noise. If they come back here to check, I'd better be history. I know you're watching, Moon. Helping me out. We make a great team. Thanks. I did good, didn't I? Stay tuned. This is just the beginning. There's much more to come, I promise.

Chapter 7

A razor-sharp shard of glass had penetrated. the thin sole of Eve's shoe and sliced upward. She screamed in shock and pain. Her face went white, but she stopped only long enough to reach down and yank the glass free. She tossed the glass aside and stumbled onward, sick and disoriented. Reeling around the corner, she struggled to get her bearings in the new passageway, its mirrors still intact.

"Ready or not, here I co-ome!" The gleeful shout came from somewhere behind her, over her right shoulder. But it was muffled, as if from a distance, and even in her panic, Eve knew she was still alone in her glass-lined alley. But close . . . the voice was close. Too close.

As was the sound of shattering glass when, to her horror, it began again. Behind her. On her right. One explosion after another. Chasing her, following her, tormenting her.

She couldn't stay ahead of it. It was happening too fast, *wham!* one panel after another, *wham!*, the glass exploding like windows in a tornado, *wham!*, so close now that a small, airborne sliver of glass caught her behind the right ear, impaling the lobe.

Eve cried out in pain again, and then her cries changed to shouts for help as she stumbled forward. Her hands fumbled along the mirrored walls, searching for a way out. Stumbling, searching, she shouted, "Help! Help me!" knowing that no one would hear her over the noise of the carnival some distance away. How could anyone hear her cries over the screaming, the shouting, the laughter, the loud music?

Why had Garth left her?

Wham! Right behind her.

She *had* to find a way out of this terrible place.

Running, stumbling, her breath coming in uneven gasps, she struggled to think clearly. Something . . . there must be something . . .

She thrust one hand into her shoulder bag while her other hand continued to probe the glass walls for an exit. Ripping a lipstick out of the depths of her purse, she yanked the top from the cylinder, freeing the greasy, deep-pink stick.

Wham!

Eve ran faster. She whirled around a corner, darted down the corridor, sped around another corner, all the while searching for a door with one hand while the other hand left a vivid slash of pink lipstick on each panel of glass as she dashed past it. She was leaving her mark, determined not to keep retracing her steps.

Wham!

The lipstick broke, as she had been afraid it would. Her hand dove back into the purse and emerged a second later with a fat, black marker. She had used it earlier to make carnival signs to post along the highway. With the marker in hand, she was careful not to miss a single panel of glass. She left behind her a thick, very visible line of black.

"Eve-ie, where are you?" the voice singsonged cheerfully. It sounded like it was further away now. *"I'm having a hard time keeping up with you! My, you are fast on your feet, aren't you? Well, I think I can fix that. Permanently."*

Wham!

The explosive sound of shattering glass behind her was too far away this time to do her any harm. Maybe her tormentor was moving in the wrong direction.

Trying to push the terrifying presence out

of her mind, Eve concentrated instead on finding a way out. She already knew that all of the
glass-strewn passageways provided no exit, so
she turned immediately away at the first sight
of shards on the floor. And the pink or black
trail she'd left behind saved her from entering
any dead-end corridors she'd already traveled.

This tiresome process led her, after what
seemed like long, anxious years, to the exit.

She was breathing hard, almost sobbing, by
the time she stumbled to the door and threw
it open. She fell out onto the porch and stood
there, clutching the wooden railing and gulping
in huge mouthfuls of cool, night air.

Darkness had fallen while she was inside. It
surrounded her, broken only by lightning
streaking the sky and the bright yellow bulbs
on the Ferris wheel towering overhead in the
distance. The music and laughter and screams
of the carnival filled her with a sudden, white-
hot rage. How dare so many people be having
a good time when she had just been tortured
and nearly killed in the Mirror Maze?

But they don't *know* that, Eve, the voice of
reason told her. No one knows. Only you and
. . . whoever.

"Whoever" could still be on her trail.

Eve pulled herself upright, took two more
deep, cleansing breaths, and staggered down

the steps toward the music and laughter.

The bored girl in the booth was gone. A CLOSED sign hung on the window. The entire area was deserted.

Eve had never felt so alone. No wonder no one had heard her shouts. There wasn't anyone there to hear them.

Afraid to take the time to wrap anything around her bleeding ankle, she hurried, in an awkward stumbling run, toward the Ferris wheel, repeatedly glancing over her shoulder for some sign of her tormentor.

She never even noticed that her hair had slipped free of its barrette and was swinging, loose and disheveled, on her shoulders.

She wasn't aware of the missing barrette until Andie, standing at a taco booth near the Ferris wheel, turned and saw Eve approaching. Her mouth dropped open, her eyes widened. Forgetting the requested taco, she ran to Eve's side.

"What on earth . . . ? Where have you been? What's wrong with you?" Her words spilled out of her mouth rapid-fire. "Hey, what happened to your hair? Wow, Eve, it's really pretty. You should wear it like that all the time. It makes you look so . . . so . . . well, different."

Renewed fury welled up inside Eve. How could Andie stand there talking about her *hair*?

Couldn't she see that something was very, very wrong?

But when Eve tried to explain, the feeling of disorientation came over her again, and all she could do was shake her head. Now that she was out of that terrible place, now that she was out in the open with music and laughter all around her, with people in a hurry to have fun brushing past her, with the smells of hot dogs and tacos and cotton candy in the air, it didn't seem possible that any of it had actually happened.

Eve looked down. Yes, there it was. Her ankle was still bleeding. And it still hurt. She touched the back of her ear and her fingers were quickly stained with blood. Proof positive that all of it had actually taken place.

Andie's eyes followed Eve's. "Oh, yuck! What'd you do? That's gross! Did you trip or something?"

Eve reached for the napkins Andie was holding. She bent to wrap them around her ankle, saying as she did so, "Have you seen Garth? He was with me in the Mirror Maze, and then he wasn't."

"Garth? That new guy? No, I haven't seen him. Is that why you took your barrette out, Eve?" Andie added coyly. "For him?"

"I didn't *take* my barrette out," Eve

snapped, standing up. "It fell out. You haven't seen him?"

Andie shook her head. "Haven't seen anyone. Serena's riding The Twister, Don and Beth and the others from the committee are making the rounds, checking things out, and Alfred was so pissed at you for being with Garth that he said, in this really disgusted voice, 'Well, I can see that *I'm* not needed around here,' and stomped off. Looked a little like one of those wooden soldiers in a Christmas pageant." She sighed. "He *is* cute, though." Then, "God, Eve, you really look terrible. You didn't go on one of those scary rides, did you? The Devil's Elbow?"

"No, Andie, I didn't go on a ride. Listen," Eve said wearily, "we need to get the committee together. Emergency meeting. The Mirror Maze is permanently out of commission and I need to tell everyone."

Andie shrugged. "It wasn't any good, anyway. Boring. And they made it too hard to get out. Who wants to hang around for hours in a gloomy old place like that?"

"Not me," Eve said grimly. Then, as they began walking, she added, "You were in the Mirror Maze?"

"Yeah, a while ago. Hated it."

"Did you see anyone else?"

"Sure. Three or four other fools, wasting their money like me. They hated it, too, although Alfred made me mad because he found his way out right away, while the rest of us were still stumbling around like idiots. He was waiting for us when we finally came out, and he looked *so* smug. I wanted to smack him." Andie turned to glance at Eve. "Why? I mean, are you asking me if I saw someone special? Like who?"

"I don't know." Just then, Don and Beth and the other committee members arrived, saying heartily that everything seemed to be running smoothly.

"Well, not really," Eve disagreed, and suggested that they all go to one of the food tents to hear what she had to say.

"You really should do something about that ankle," Andie said. "Those napkins look disgusting."

Blood from the wound had soaked through, making a sticky mess. "I will," Eve promised, "as soon as I fill everyone in on what's happened."

They were halfway to the tent when she spotted Garth, talking to Serena and Alfred at the archery booth. The second Garth saw her, he was at her side. His eyes quickly took in the hair, the awkward, clearly painful walk, then the bloody napkin swathing her ankle.

"What happened?" he asked. "Where did you go?"

"Where did *I* go?" Eve looked up at him defiantly, suddenly very, very angry with him for deserting her. "*I* didn't go anywhere! You were the one who left." She was aware of people watching them with interest, but she didn't care. "Without a word."

"You left first!" Garth protested over the loud music and shrieks from the rides. "You went so fast, you got ahead of me and turned a corner. Out of sight, just like that. Before I could catch up to you, you called back 'I'm out of here.' By the time I turned the corner, you were gone. How come you didn't wait for me?"

"I never told you I was leaving," Eve argued. "How could I? I couldn't find the way out. And if I *had* found the way out, I wouldn't have left. I'd have waited for you."

The color in Garth's cheeks deepened. "I *did* hear you say you were leaving," he insisted. "And when I finally found my own way out, you weren't anywhere around, and no one had seen you."

"Sure," Eve said brusquely. "Listen, forget it. No big deal!" She was too tired to deal with this now, and besides, she couldn't stand the satisfied smirk on Alfred's face as he watched them argue. "Right now, I've got to tell everyone what happened in the maze. You're not a member of the committee," she added stiffly, "but if you want to come along, I can't stop you."

"Oh, I'm coming, all right," Garth said emphatically. "We're not finished with this. And I want to know what happened to you in there. You look . . . pretty bad."

Was Garth telling the truth about what had happened in the maze? Eve wondered.

Or had he suggested going in the maze just so he could terrorize her?

Chapter 8

Eve had just finished telling her story to the committee and Garth when the blonde girl from the Mirror Maze ticket booth burst into the food tent and shouted, "There she is! That's her!" She was pointing directly at Eve, who was standing at the head of a table, the committee members seated in a semicircle in front of her.

Heads swiveled toward the front of the tent.

There were two campus police officers behind the girl. The three marched straight toward Eve. "What did you use?" the girl demanded when she was facing Eve. "A hammer? An axe handle? I've never seen such a mess!" Turning toward one of the policemen, she ordered, "Arrest her! She and that guy," pointing toward Garth, "were the last ones who went into the maze. I figured they'd left, so I closed the booth and went to get something to eat. When I came back and looked inside, there it was, half the mirrors shattered and glass all over the place. *She* did it!"

"I did not!" Eve said heatedly, conscious of heads on the opposite side of the huge tent turning toward them in curiosity. "I don't know who it was. I didn't see anyone. Look," pointing toward her napkin-wrapped ankle, "I got cut. And there's another cut on my ear. Would I do that to myself?"

The girl sniffed in disdain. "Probably happened while you were going crazy smashing all those mirrors."

Alfred jumped to his feet. "This is stupid," he said. "Eve wouldn't wreck anything at the carnival. She's in charge of this committee. Nobody wants this thing to be a success more than Eve does. If she says it was someone else, it was someone else."

Eve glanced at him uncertainly. She was grateful for the support, but she had wanted it to come from Garth, and he wasn't saying a word. Neither was anyone else on the committee. Serena looked blank and Andie looked confused. After a moment, Garth got up and left the tent.

Watching him go, Eve wondered if she would ever see him again. But if he wasn't going to stand up for her, she didn't really care. She turned her attention to the girl from the booth.

"You've got a lot of nerve accusing me," she said. "Anyone could have gone into that maze when you left. That's why," she added pointedly, "you aren't *supposed* to leave unless you get someone to take your place. Didn't anyone explain that to you?"

"I was hungry." The girl turned her back on Eve and said to the police officer on her left, "Well? Aren't you going to arrest her? Or is vandalism suddenly no longer a crime?"

"Look, miss," he said politely, "it's already been established that you were absent from the booth for a period of time. Like your friend here says," waving a hand in Eve's direction, "anyone could have gone into that maze while you were gone. We've got no proof that she was the one who did it."

"Are you *sure* you didn't see anyone else?" Eve pressed. Not because she was anxious to clear herself. It didn't look like the police officers were going to arrest her. But she was anxious to find out who had been in that maze with her. To find out who that soft, sinister voice belonged to.

"Oh, cut the act!" the girl said with scorn. "You know you did it, and I know you did it. But since I can't prove it . . ." Shaking her head in disgust and anger, she turned and stomped away.

"So," Alfred said, coming over to stand beside Eve, "what kind of damage are we talking here? Shouldn't we all go take a look? See if the maze can be salvaged?"

"It can't," Eve said firmly. "It would be too expensive, and we're not making that much money on it, anyway. But," addressing the police officers, "whoever that was in the maze was after *me*. He called me by name." Remembering the terrifying chase through the maze, the *whams* racing along behind her, she shuddered. "He came in there to find *me*."

Before the police officers had digested this new information, Garth returned, a first-aid kit in hand. He marched straight over to Eve and ordered her to sit down in a chair, "while I take a look at that foot. I've had some first-aid training. If I can't patch you up, you're going to the infirmary."

He hadn't abandoned her, after all. He was, in fact, the only person who had been concerned about her injuries.

When the foot had been bandaged and Garth had daubed antiseptic on the cut behind her ear, the two campus police officers led all of them back to the Mirror Maze.

Everyone but Eve seemed stunned by the destruction.

"You were in the middle of all this?" Alfred said in awe, staring at Eve. Garth's mouth was grim, Serena had tears of disbelief in her eyes, and Andie's face was white with shock. "I can't believe you weren't sliced to ribbons," she whispered to Eve.

Eve answered all of the questions directed at her in an amazingly calm voice, until one policeman asked her if she knew anyone who was angry with her.

That stumped her. Could someone be so angry with her that they'd chase her down a corridor, smashing mirrors in her face, taunting her the whole way? What could she have done to make someone so mad?

She couldn't think of anything.

She shook her head. "No. I don't think so."

"Well, if anything else happens, let us know," the younger police officer said.

Eve stared at him in dismay. "Anything else?" she said, her voice cracking slightly. "You think something else might happen?"

He shrugged. "This looks like serious business to me," he said. "Like your friend said, you could have been seriously injured. And you said he knew your name. Might be a good idea to stay close to your dorm room for a while, until we get to the bottom of this."

"I'm cochair of this event," she said, trying to keep her voice level. "The other chairperson is already in the infirmary. That leaves me. I can't run things from my dorm room." Why didn't they just *catch* whoever had done this? Wasn't that their job?

"We'll keep an eye on her," Garth told the police officer. "You just find out who did this, okay? Then she won't have to worry."

Leaving the officers there to search the scene thoroughly, Eve led the way out of the maze. It wasn't difficult, thanks to her lipstick and marker trail. But she made very sure that the group stayed close together until they reached the exit.

The skies had opened up while they were inside. It was pouring thick sheets of rain that were rapidly turning the earth to mud and sending people running for the exits in droves.

"Of course," Eve said wearily as they clustered under the building's overhang, "of course it's raining. Why wouldn't it be?" And wondered why she hadn't let Alfred or Serena or Andie or one of the townspeople run this stupid event.

If someone was so furious with her that they wanted to hurt her, then she needed to be tougher and stronger. Like her mother.

The trouble was, she didn't know if she had it in her.

Eve stood up straighter, took a deep breath. She wasn't going to fold, not yet. She had faked being organized and responsible, hadn't she? Maybe she could fake the rest. She'd pretend she wasn't scared half out of her wits, pretend that she was as much in control as she'd always seemed to be, pretend that she hadn't realized the maniac in the maze knew exactly who she was and was out to get her.

Maybe she'd do such a good job, she'd even fool *herself* into thinking she wasn't scared half to death.

It was worth a try.

Besides, rain or no rain, she still had the carnival to think about. People were counting on her.

"This place is going to be a mess tomorrow," Serena commented grimly as they all stood in a group, watching the sheets of rain.

Eve laughed bitterly. "Could it be any worse than it was today?" she cried. "I don't know about anybody else, but I'm starving, and I don't want any of the junk food here. I say we all head for Vinnie's and forget about this stupid carnival for a little while."

"Are you sure?" Garth asked, gazing down

into her rain-streaked face. "You don't want to head for the dorm? That ankle must be hurting."

"No! My room is boring!" Eve cried giddily. "Come on, let's go! Vinnie's isn't that far. And a little rain never killed anyone." Unlike a million pieces of flying, broken glass, she thought instantly.

When they were settled in Garth's car, daubing at wet faces with crumpled tissues yanked from pockets, Eve, sitting in the front between Garth and Alfred, leaned her head against the seat and wondered who could be so angry with her, they wanted her to die.

At Vinnie's, crowded because of the rain, she knew she was talking and laughing too loudly. She felt the stares of Serena and Alfred and Andie as she chattered away, her words spilling out of her in a rush in her effort to pretend she wasn't scared. She couldn't help it. If she kept talking and laughing and pretending that everything was okay, maybe everything would *seem* okay.

Garth didn't know her well enough to realize she was behaving oddly. Still, when they'd talked earlier, at the carnival, she must have struck him as a quieter person, because she felt his eyes on her once or twice and, when she looked up, she saw the concern in them.

He knew something was wrong.

That wasn't what Eve wanted. She wanted everyone to think there was *nothing* wrong. That she wasn't scared. That she had passed off the maze incident with barely a shudder. That she wasn't still thinking about it.

She calmed down then, deciding that a better approach would be to act as she always did. Calm, with no outward hint that she was terrified. Composed, as if she knew exactly what she was doing and how to do it. That shouldn't be hard. Hadn't she been doing it all of her life? What was so different about this time?

Are you kidding? the answer came readily. The difference, Eve Forsythe, is that you're not just running a social event this time. You *thought* that's what you were doing. But you were wrong. *Dead* wrong. This time, you're running for your *life*.

Serena and Alfred lived off-campus, at Nightingale Hall, an old, brick building with a sagging front porch. Surrounded by huge, old, dark-limbed oak trees that kept the house shadowed even on sunny days, Nightingale Hall sat high on a hill overlooking the highway. Nicknamed Nightmare Hall by the students, partly because of its gloomy appearance but mostly because of stories about strange happenings there, it seemed to Eve to sink deeper and deeper into its surroundings with every passing day, as if one day she would drive by there and the house would have disappeared from sight completely, with only the top of its brick chimney poking up over the crest of the hill.

She didn't see how anyone could live there. But when Garth dropped them off that night, Serena and Alfred jumped from the car and ran up the driveway like anyone else going back to the place where they lived.

It had stopped raining by the time they returned to campus. The sky was cloudless, the moon, almost full now, shining down upon them. The air smelled clean and fresh and the ground didn't seem to be oozing mud the way Eve had feared. Maybe the carnival grounds would be dry when the site opened the next afternoon.

She would have to remember to put an OUT OF ORDER sign on the Mirror Maze first thing tomorrow.

Exhausted, she showered, rebandaged her ankle, and went to bed. She was asleep almost immediately.

Meanwhile, a figure stood motionless behind the darkened Ferris wheel.

The figure's arms were outstretched and raised toward the sky. Its eyes were closed, its face upturned, as if it were basking in the silvery glow of the moon.

Chapter 9

I could have killed Eve tonight. She ran too fast, though. Besides, it was fun scaring her, chasing her, smashing those mirrors while she ran. So I made up my mind not to kill her just yet. But then I was disappointed when she got out, because I was having so much fun. She's smart, Eve is. That was clever, the bit with the lipstick and the marker.

But she's not clever enough to figure out that I get my power from you, Moon. She'd never believe it. She'd laugh. Make fun of me. I can just hear her. "Oh, get real," she'd say, in that scornful way she has. When I didn't back down, she'd add, "Special power? You and the moon? And what planet did you say you were from?" Eve doesn't believe in anything that she can't see right in front of her eyes. And she doesn't want anyone else to believe, either. Of all the people in parapsychology class who don't belong there, she's the worst. The most logical, the most cynical, the most scornful.

Never mind. She'll learn. I saw the look on her face tonight. She's pretending not to be scared, but it's not working. I could see the fear in her eyes. Maybe no one else could, but it was there. That fear is there because what happened to her doesn't make any sense. Eve is terrified of anything that can't be explained logically. That's really why she's afraid. Because she just doesn't understand.

I wonder what she'll think when she realizes, as she will soon enough, that she's not the only target. Others made fun, too, and like her, they must be punished. Will she be relieved when someone else suffers instead of her? Or will she be even more terrified? I wonder. It'll be fun finding out. Seeing what she's really made of.

Time is crucial, right? I mean, you up there, you're only at your fullest for a little while, which means I'm only at my best for a little while. No time to waste. My goal is to teach them that they shouldn't overlook me. Someone as special as I am should not be ignored. They are also going to learn not to make fun of things they don't understand.

They will either learn that, or they'll die trying.

Chapter 10

On Monday morning, the second thing Eve did after neatly making her bed was pull her hair away from her face and fasten it tightly with a barrette. Because Andie had said she looked "different" with it loose. She didn't want to look different. Not now. She needed to look the same, act the same, *be* the same, if she was going to get through this week.

Eve's first class on Mondays was parapsychology. Alfred was waiting for her in the doorway, as always, and took a seat beside her, opposite Serena, who was reading a magazine, and behind Andie, who was putting the finishing touches on her weekly letter to her father. She had left the room before Eve that morning so she could stop at the university post office and buy stamps.

Eve had enjoyed the walk alone. It was a beautiful morning. There wasn't a cloud in the blue sky overhead and only a gentle breeze stirred the branches of the huge old trees lining the campus walkways. She hoped the sun was drying up the mud at the carnival site. The grounds didn't open until two o'clock. That should be enough time.

The episode in the Mirror Maze seemed unreal in the bright morning sunshine. If it hadn't been for the bandage on her ankle, Eve would have been convinced that she'd imagined the whole thing.

If the police had discovered anything important in their search of the maze, they would have called her. They hadn't. So she still didn't have a single clue to the identity of the glass-smasher who had called her by name.

She groaned inwardly when she walked down the hall and saw Alfred standing in the doorway. Why didn't he just give up? She had given no sign, ever, that she was interested in him as anything more than a friend, yet he continued to hover over her like a lovesick bird. He called often, sent her little notes, bought candy bars for her at the bookstore and brought them to class, usually handing them to her in front of everyone so they could see his devotion.

"Well, *I* think he's cute," Andie had said

when Eve complained. "If you don't want him, I'll take him."

Cute? Alfred? Never. All of his features were in the right place, but he was too stiff, too polished, for "cute." He was like a brand-new Ken doll. And Eve Forsythe was no Barbie.

"Dr. Litton," Andie asked as class began, "why do I always have weird dreams when the moon is full?"

Snickers of derision rippled around the room.

But the professor, a tall, attractive woman with graying hair worn in a long, thick French braid, nodded. "I've heard that before." She glanced around the room. "How many of you believe that the phases of the moon affect us in one way or another?"

About half the class raised a hand. Three of the hands belonged to Alfred, Andie, and Serena. If Kevin had been there instead of in the infirmary, Eve felt sure his hand would have been up, too.

Her own hands stayed on her desk. It wasn't logical to believe that the moon could make people dream, or make them do anything else. She'd seen the werewolf movies, read the books. She thought it was all very silly. Men didn't turn into wolves under a full moon or any kind of moon, and no one fell in love because of a round, silver ball up in the sky. She had never believed for a moment that the moon was anything but the earth's satellite.

And she didn't have weird dreams when the moon was full.

Other people did, it turned out, and they all began describing them while Dr. Litton listened attentively.

Those who thought it was all nonsense said so, including Eve, and the discussion became very lively.

It was still going on when class was dismissed.

"Hey, Andie," a tall, husky, blond boy teased as they all left their desks, "the man in the moon is coming to get you tonight. Better watch out!"

Andie flushed and retorted, "You're the one who'd better watch out, Boomer. A closed mind is a dying mind. If a fresh, new thought ever forced its way into that dried-up, shrunken little brain of yours, your entire body would go into shock."

"The moon affects the tides," Serena said to no one in particular. "How do we know it doesn't affect us, too?"

They were still arguing when Eve spotted a

tall, dark-haired figure lounging against the wall opposite the open classroom door. Garth.

Eve picked up her books and left with the rest of the class. Not sure that Garth actually was waiting for her, she intended to simply give him a casual wave as she walked by. But he joined her before she had a chance to wave, erasing any uncertainty.

A glum Alfred remained stubbornly at Eve's side, glaring at Garth.

Ignoring Alfred as they all walked down the hall, Garth said to Eve, "I just wanted to make sure we were okay. I mean, we never finished our discussion last night, did we? I'd have hung around, but you looked like you really needed to crash in your room. Feeling better?"

"You don't have to worry about her," Alfred said before Eve could answer. "She *has* people to look out for her."

Eve shot him an irritated look. "I don't need *anyone* looking out for me," she said, forgetting for the moment that the previous afternoon in the maze she would have been grateful for just that. "I can take care of myself." To Garth, she said, "I'm fine. Thanks for asking. Why aren't you at work?"

"I have Mondays off. I thought maybe you could use some help at the carnival this afternoon. And I wanted to know if you'd heard anything from the police about the maze. Did they find anything? Any clues?"

Although they had just left the building and walked out into bright sunshine and a beautiful, balmy day, Eve felt a chill down her spine when Garth mentioned the maze. "Nope. Nothing yet. I guess they'll call me when they know something."

They walked in silence across the Commons, a wide, green expanse of lawn where a few students were tossing Frisbees. Behind them, Andie and Serena continued to argue heatedly with Boomer and his friends about the effect of a full moon on earthlings.

"You don't believe in anything that you can't see with your own eyes?" Andie was saying in a loud voice. "Well, I haven't seen you actually *make* a touchdown yet, Boomer."

Loud hoots and laughter at Boomer's expense followed.

"What's all the arguing about?" Garth asked as they approached the science building where Eve's next class was held.

"Nothing," Eve answered. "Nothing important, anyway. It's leftover from our parapsychology class. Some of them think paranormal stuff is actually normal. We argue about it all the time."

Garth hummed the *Twilight Zone* theme

song. "You mean like someone bending metal spoons with their mind, and ESP, stuff like that?"

Eve nodded, and glanced over at him as they arrived at the art building. "You don't believe in that stuff, do you?"

"I believe in everything. Until someone proves to me that it's not possible. And no one's done that yet." He grinned down at her. "Are you about to do it now? Enlighten me?"

"No. I don't care enough about any of it to prove that it doesn't exist." Afraid that she had sounded too much like her mother again, Eve hastily added, "I mean, I've got a lot of other stuff to think about right now."

"So, I repeat my offer to help. I'll be back at two. Meet you on the grounds, in front of the Ferris wheel." Garth glanced up at the sky. "It's not going to rain. That's a good omen, right?"

Eve frowned. Omens again. What *was* it with people? Why couldn't they just deal with reality? So it wasn't going to rain. The only thing that meant was that they weren't going to get wet. And yes, that was a good thing. But it wasn't a sign that the carnival was going to be a raging success. There was a lot more to running the Founders' Day celebration than weather.

"We don't need you," Alfred insisted as Garth turned to leave.

"I didn't say you did. I just said I'd be there. And I will."

When he had gone, Alfred held the door open for Eve, saying, "What are you letting him hang around for? He's not even on the committee."

"In case you've forgotten, Alfred," Eve said firmly, "we were rained out early last night. That's not good. We lost money. We need to make that up today if we're going to come out ahead. So I'm not turning down any offers for help."

After her classes, she stopped at the infirmary to check on Kevin. He was still bruised and sore, but promised he'd be back on his feet by Wednesday. "How'd class go this morning?" he asked.

Eve knew he was talking about Dr. Litton's class. He hated missing it.

Eve sat in a wooden chair beside Kevin's bed. "The usual. Andie started an argument about the moon, of all things. You can borrow my notes if you want."

"Ah, the full moon. I saw it through my window last night. Not quite there, but almost." He smiled knowingly at Eve. "No need to ask which side you were on. The side of practical reality, no doubt."

Eve wasn't sure why that stung, but it did. "You make being practical sound almost like a crime," she snapped.

"Not a crime. It's just . . . well, you never know, Eve. Maybe it's a mistake to dismiss things you don't understand until you've explored them some."

Almost exactly what Garth had said. Kevin would like Garth. "The only thing I'm going to explore right now," she said, standing up, "is the carnival site. We need a really good afternoon, so keep your fingers crossed, okay?"

He grinned up at her. "Just a silly superstitition?"

Eve couldn't help laughing. She told him to get better fast, waved, and left.

Just as she'd hoped, the sun had dried the mud from last night's rain. Maybe that *was* a good sign.

Taking a deep breath, she hurried over to the Mirror Maze and, hands shaking slightly, hung an OUT OF ORDER sign on the booth. Then she turned quickly and hurried away.

The afternoon was a rousing success for the Founders' Day carnival. Beautiful weather brought both students and townspeople out in huge numbers. Eve stayed busy making the rounds, checking to make sure there was enough food in the food booths, money for change at the game booths, and that the rides were in working order.

Garth showed up shortly after two, and Eve didn't complain when he made the rounds with her. It gave them a chance to talk, and she was pretty sure no one would try to hurt her while Garth was at her side.

The afternoon went by quickly. The committee met in the food tent at twilight to eat a quick meal and discuss any problems. There were none. The crowds were good, the weather perfect, and only a handful of people had complained about the Mirror Maze being shut down.

Over coffee, Eve felt herself relaxing. Maybe it *was* going to be a success, after all. Maybe they'd make enough money to make a huge donation to Alice's scholarship fund.

When they finished dinner, she was able to say, "Back to work!" cheerfully. "I want to check out the games again. Don's manning the dart booth, and he was worried about running out of prizes."

Alfred and Garth wanted to go with her, but Eve was getting tired of being escorted everywhere. She felt relaxed enough to dismiss them, telling them she had better things for them to do. She sent Alfred to the Ferris wheel to make sure all was well, and Garth to the Devil's Elbow. Both protested, but Eve ignored them. She wasn't a child. She didn't need protectors.

Serena promised to check the food booths now that the evening crowd was arriving, and Andie went off to freshen her makeup, promising to meet Eve at the dart booth. Eve struck out across the carnival grounds on her own.

Darkness had fallen while they were in the food tent. The garish yellow bulbs on the Ferris wheel spun around in a hazy glow, and the nearly full moon lit up a black velvet sky. Laughter and music and the smell of hot dogs, popcorn, and cotton candy filled the air around her as Eve made her way to the dart booth. A clown, dressed in the same costume Garth had worn the day before, passed her, carrying a huge bouquet of brightly colored balloons. People called out as she went by, "Great carnival, Eve!" "Good job, Eve!" She'd heard those words many times before, and they gave her the same sense of warmth they always had.

But . . . this was only Monday. The whole week lay ahead of her, stretching out in front of her like a sleeping snake, peaceful enough now but ready to strike at any moment.

There was a large, noisy crowd in front of the dart booth. Inside, Boomer, the football player who had argued with Andie that morning, was taking his turn playing "target." He was standing at the rear of the booth with an apple on his head. The darts had harmless, rubber suction tips. If the customer's aim was accurate, the apple would have as many as five thick black darts protruding from it.

Boomer's huge bulk nearly filled the booth. Eve had had to promise to help him with two term papers to get him to participate. He was laughing now, the shiny red apple perched on the top of his blond head.

Reluctant to push through the crowd, Eve went around instead to the back of the booth and lifted the canvas flap.

She crouched near the ground, afraid that if she stood up, she'd distract the customer, a boy named Tony Paris.

Tony concentrated on his aim. The first four darts he threw smacked into the apple and held. The crowd of friends around him cheered. One more successful throw, and he'd win a prize.

Tony raised his arm to take aim again.

Eve watched as the fifth dart hit the air. Its aim seemed accurate. It was heading straight for Boomer who, taunting Tony, stood perfectly still, his powerful body a can't-miss target against the canvas.

Eve peered more closely. There was something wrong.

There were *two* darts aiming straight at Boomer.

But . . . one had no round, fat suction cup on its tip. And what was there instead made Eve's blood stop flowing.

A metal tip. She saw, heading straight for Boomer, a sharp, wicked-looking, pointed metal tip, the very kind she'd been so careful not to order. "No," she had told the carnival supply people, "not *that* kind. Not real darts. We want the other kind, the rubber suction cup-tipped ones. We don't want anyone getting hurt."

"We don't want anyone getting hurt" . . . she *had* said that. She clearly remembered saying that.

But someone was going to get hurt, anyway.

Eve opened her mouth to scream, knowing it was already too late.

Chapter 11

It *was* too late.

Even as Eve opened her mouth to scream a warning, even as Boomer realized that there were two missiles flying toward him and that one was not what it was supposed to be, the metal point, sharp as an icepick, slammed into the middle of his chest. It penetrated his thin white T-shirt, impaling itself just above his rib cage.

At the same time, Tony's harmless rubber-tipped dart slapped up against the apple. But no one was looking at it. All eyes were on Boomer's chest.

There were gasps and shrieks from the crowd. Then shock struck everyone dumb and an appalled silence fell.

A tiny spot of bright red encircled the dart protruding from Boomer's chest and began spreading.

He looked down, the expression on his face one of total bewilderment. The apple rolled off his head and fell to the ground, bouncing several times before it rolled to rest at Eve's feet. Still open-mouthed, her eyes left Boomer and focused on the apple, as if it might have some answers for her.

It didn't.

When she pulled herself to her feet and looked at Boomer again, he was still standing. His face wore that same hurt, bewildered look, but his skin was ashen. He placed his hands around the dart gently, carefully, as if he needed to make sure that it was actually implanted in his body. Then he swayed, just a little, took a half-step backward, and slowly, like someone deciding they've been standing long enough and might like to sit down for a while now, slid to a sitting position on the ground, his back against the canvas.

Eve ran to him, knelt beside him, took his wrist, feeling for a pulse. When she found it, it was weak and thready.

"Don't remove the dart!" a voice she recognized as Garth's warned from behind her. "Leave it in place. If you take it out, he could bleed to death."

Eve had no intention of removing the dart. She could no more have pulled it from Boomer's chest than she could have put it there in the first place. "Ambulance," she whispered to Garth, and he barked the order over his shoulder.

The crowd of witnesses began shouting then, and pushing and shoving to see over the counter. Other people, noticing the commotion, joined them, until the crowd had swollen to three times its original size. In a fog of shock, her heart pounding in fear for Boomer, Eve half-heard questions being tossed back and forth. "What's going on? Who's hurt? Is that Boomer? Oh, God, he's bleeding! What happened? Is he dead?"

Tony, the boy who had been throwing darts when Boomer was struck kept shouting, "I didn't do it, I didn't! See, the darts *I* threw are still stuck to the apple, see? The dart that hit Boomer came from somewhere else."

Eve kept her hand on Boomer's wrist. As long as she could feel that pulse, feel the blood pumping through his veins, she could tell herself that she was holding onto his life, refusing to let it slip away. His eyes were still open, staring straight ahead, but they were vacant, reminding Eve of the glass eyes on her dolls when she was little.

The wound was so close to Boomer's heart. Too close.

"Where is that ambulance?" she hissed to Garth. Several of the committee members, including Andie and Alfred, had joined them inside the booth, drawn there by the crowd and the noise. Serena hovered near the counter, upset but trying to disperse the onlookers. They ignored her.

A doctor who had been enjoying the carnival with his family arrived, his black bag in hand, and after shaking his head grimly, wrapped a blood-pressure cuff around Boomer's upper left arm. When he had taken a reading, he shook his graying head again and was about to speak when the shrill wail of the ambulance split the air.

The crowd did part, then, to make way for the emergency vehicle, which drove across the carnival grounds straight to the dart booth.

"He's not going to die, is he?" Eve anxiously asked the doctor as the injured Salem University athlete was loaded into the ambulance. "I mean, he's really strong and healthy. That will help, won't it?"

"It might," was the doctor's cryptic answer. He climbed into the ambulance with the patient.

Eve asked the same question of the attendant as he slammed and locked the doors. All she would say was, "Can't say. Stand back, please."

When the ambulance had pulled away, its siren shrieking to prove there was no time to waste, Eve sagged against the dart booth's counter. A handful of suction cup-tipped darts lay on her left. But there was blood on her blouse and skirt, proof that there had been a different kind of dart in the booth.

She turned her white, strained face toward Garth. "Where did that dart come from?" she asked softly. She picked up one of the rubber-tipped darts, held it up for everyone around her to see. "*These* are the ones we're using. These are the ones we ordered. I know, because I'm the one who ordered them." She scanned the crowd. "Did anyone see who threw that metal dart?"

There were murmurs and mutterings and the shaking of heads. No one had seen anything unusual. They had all been watching Boomer, laughing as he set himself up as a target. No one had noticed a hand lifting into the air, aiming the deadly metal point straight at Boomer's heart. As far as the spectators were concerned, the vicious projectile had come out of nowhere.

But the campus police officers who arrived on the scene would allow no one to leave until their questions had been asked and answered.

By the time the crowd was released, it was dark. The huge, silver moon stared down upon them, as if, an exhausted Eve thought wearily, it was accusing them. How could you let this happen? she imagined the moon saying to her. How could you be so careless? That boy will probably die, you know.

"The police will find out where that dart came from," Alfred said, putting a comforting arm around Eve's shoulders as they left the booth. "It'll have fingerprints or a brand name on it. Something. They'll find something."

Eve slipped out from under the arm. "I don't think so," she disagreed. "I don't think there will be any fingerprints at all, or any brand name. I don't think the police will discover one single thing about that dart. Whoever threw it will see to that."

"Well, one thing's for sure," Garth said, ignoring Alfred's angry look, "this wasn't any accident. You don't aim a dart like that straight at someone's heart out of carelessness." He turned to Eve as they passed beneath the Ferris wheel. Many people had deserted the carnival when the ambulance arrived, and most of the seats on the yellow wheel were empty. "Maybe it was the same person who broke all those mirrors in the maze yesterday," he added. "At least you weren't the target this time."

"Unless," Alfred said, fixing a cool gaze on Eve, "the dart-thrower was really aiming for Eve. I mean, you *were* in the booth, too, right?"

"Yes, but . . ."

Alfred shrugged. "Maybe he was aiming for you, and someone bumped his arm or something."

"If that had happened," Serena said, "the person who'd done the bumping would have noticed something, and remembered, and told the police. I think Boomer was the target, not Eve. Quit trying to scare her, Alfred."

"I wasn't!" he protested, his face flushing an ugly red. "But if someone's after her, she should know it, shouldn't she? It seems pretty obvious to me that Eve could have been the one in that ambulance instead of Boomer."

The thought made Eve ill. She was a lot thinner than Boomer. That dart probably would have killed her instantly.

They went into the food tent and collapsed on benches. "I can't believe," Eve said slowly, her head in her hands, "that no one saw anything. In that huge crowd, not one person saw who threw that dart?"

"It's as if that dart came out of nowhere," Garth said.

"No," Eve shook her head. "It didn't come out of nowhere. Things don't just appear out of nowhere. That dart came from someone's hand. It shot straight out of the hand of someone nasty and vicious and cruel." She sank into gloomy thought then, not touching the plate of snacks Serena placed on the table a few minutes later.

"Boomer was making fun of parapsychology this morning," Alfred said suddenly. "Maybe someone was mad at him for that."

Eve laughed harshly. "Oh, Alfred, get real! No one would try to kill Boomer just because he doesn't believe all that garbage. That's ridiculous!"

Stung, Alfred shot back, "Well, *you* were attacked yesterday in the Mirror Maze, weren't you? Hasn't it crossed your mind that you make fun of the stuff in that class more than anyone else? You sneer at practically everything Dr. Litton says. Maybe you should give that some thought, Eve, instead of calling me ridiculous!" And he jumped up and hurried from the tent, his back stiffer than usual.

"Wow," Andie breathed, watching him go, "I've never seen Alfred so mad. You weren't very nice to him, Eve. You shouldn't have hurt his feelings. You know how he feels about you." Then she stood up and, without saying good-bye, followed Alfred out of the tent.

Eve shook her head. "I've had better days. Like that Tuesday last fall when I had a really nasty root canal."

Garth glanced pointedly toward the roof of the tent. The glow of the moon was visible through the hole at the tent pole. "Maybe a full moon makes people do crazy things."

Eve flew up off the bench. "Don't *you* start that crap! I don't want to hear a word about the moon or the sun or the stars or people bending spoons with their minds. Not *one word*!" She was shouting, and heads passing by the tent turned in her direction. She was instantly mortified. "I'm sorry," she whispered, "I'm sorry," and, like Alfred and Andie before her, ran from the tent.

Boomer, she thought as she ran, Boomer. Are you alive or dead? How could that happen so fast? One second, you were standing there taunting Tony about how he couldn't hit Mount Rushmore even if he was standing on top of it, and the next second, you were sliding to the floor with blood on your T-shirt and all of the light fading from your eyes. How? Why? I don't understand.

Eve knew she shouldn't be leaving the carnival site. She was supposed to be in charge, and the games and rides would be open for another two hours. But she wanted desperately to get away from there, away from the music and the noise and the smells, and hide somewhere safe. There were eight other committee members besides her and Kevin. Let them take over the responsibility. Maybe if they did, no one else would get hurt.

But the old habits of so many years slowed her steps. She had never turned over the reins to anything in her life, had never shirked a single chore, never failed to discharge her duties responsibly and well. How could she do it now?

It wasn't Kevin's fault that he was in the infirmary. He was counting on her to keep things going until he got back. The *school* was counting on her. And there was the scholarship in Alice's name . . .

She was just about to turn around and go back when a voice whispered from somewhere close to her, *"Eve! Where are you going, Eve? Running away, are we? That's pretty cowardly, if you ask me."*

Eve froze. She was standing in the shadow of the ticket booth for the most challenging ride at the carnival, aptly named The Snake. Unlike steep roller-coasters, the ride was placed on metal tracks set relatively close to the ground. But its red and green cars sped along on a torturous route that snapped backward and forward so suddenly and at such sharp angles, complaints of whiplash echoed as people climbed weakly from the cars at the end of a ride. Still, The Snake was popular.

Quiet now, the cars sat just beyond the booth, awaiting customers. Its music, a pounding rock song, continued to play, but Eve saw no one inside the booth waiting to sell tickets.

"You're running because you don't understand what happened to Boomer, aren't you?" the whisper continued.

Eve's head swiveled, her eyes searching. She was at the far end of the carnival, almost to the exit, and the lighting wasn't as strong as it was in the heart of the grounds. She saw nothing, no one. Either everyone who wanted to had already ridden The Snake, or the crowds had thinned more than she'd thought after Boomer's accident.

"You just can't stand it when you don't understand something, can you, Eve? You hate it when you can't come up with a logical, sensible explanation for something. What a tiny little mind you have."

Eve began to back away from the booth. It

seemed to be the only place close at hand capable of hiding the disembodied voice. "What do you want?" she managed to whisper.

"*You. I want you, Eve. And I'm going to get you. Just like I got Boomer, another unbeliever.*" A soft, evil laugh. "*He's dead, you know. Never even made it to the hospital alive. My aim was perfect, thanks to the power. You shouldn't have been so contemptuous of the power of the moon today, Eve. You have no idea how strong that power can be. And I get to share in it, because I'm special. More special than you could ever hope to be. Boomer would testify to that . . . if he could.*"

"You're crazy!" Eve shouted, continuing to back away, her eyes still darting into the darkness seeking some sign of her tormentor. "You're just plain crazy! The moon is just the moon, that's all it is! You'd better get yourself to a shrink, fast!"

Then she turned and ran, as fast as her bandaged ankle would allow. But instead of racing onward, to the safety of her dorm room, she ran back the way she had come, deeper into the carnival, until she reached the food tent where she had left Garth and Serena.

She burst into the tent, breathing hard, her face pale and shiny with sweat, her eyes wide with fear.

Garth and Serena were gone, their bench empty.

Despairing, Eve turned, and walked straight into Alfred.

"Eve?" he said. "What's wrong?"

Chapter 12

As upset as she was, Eve couldn't bring herself to share what had happened to her with Alfred. He'd take advantage of it. That was who he was. He wanted to be in charge of something . . . some*one*. All she'd have to do was show the tiniest sign of weakness and Alfred would dive in for the kill, ready to take over.

He had told her once that he'd always wanted a puppy when he was growing up, but his mother wouldn't let him have any pets at all, "not even a hamster." Maybe that was why he seemed to be looking for someone to protect. He'd been sent off to boarding school when he was a teenager, and that must have been lonely for him. She didn't think he made friends easily. Maybe no one had ever depended on Alfred. The only thing Eve was really sure about was, if she confided in Alfred now about the evil, threatening voice she'd just heard, he would be welded to her side like a Siamese twin. That wasn't what she wanted. She wasn't about to become the needy little puppy that Alfred had always wanted.

"Do you know where Garth and Serena went?" she asked instead. "Have you seen Andie?"

"No, and no. But I have good news." Alfred followed her out of the tent. "Boomer's going to be okay. I called the hospital. He might not play football next fall, but barring complications, he's going to live."

Eve stared at Alfred. "No," she said softly, "that's not true. You're lying. Boomer's dead. I know he is. You're just trying to make me feel better."

It was Alfred's turn to look startled. "What? Are you nuts? I wouldn't lie about a thing like that. He's *not* dead. He's going to be fine. What's the matter with you?"

He wasn't lying, she could tell. Boomer *was* alive.

Eve closed her eyes and sagged against the wall of the food tent. The voice oozing out of the booth just now had lied to her. It'd said those words just to torment her, torture her, just for fun!

"Eve?" Alfred bent his head close to hers.

"You look like you need to sit down. Here, lean on me."

Eve struggled to take in the information he'd just fed her. Boomer was alive! And he was going to be okay. They didn't have another death on their hands. On her conscience. Her knees went so weak with relief, it would have made sense to lean on Alfred's extended arm. Instead, Eve stiffened her back and stood up straight. Some of the color returned to her face. "No, thanks," she said politely. "I'm not going to collapse, Alfred. That's good news you gave me, not bad. I'm okay, really."

"Am I interrupting something?" Andie's voice asked coolly as she arrived on the scene.

She wasn't smiling. That was the first thing Eve noticed when she looked up. The second thing she noticed was that Andie looked a little frazzled herself. Her hair, always unruly, seemed even more chaotic than usual, and her cheeks were flushed. There was a small rip in the hem of her T-shirt, and the knees of her jeans were dirty.

"What happened to you?" Eve asked, moving slightly away from Alfred. She could imagine how the scene must have looked to Andie, coming upon Eve and Alfred with their heads so close together. And thought, Why can't Andie realize that if I could, I'd make a gift of Alfred to her? It's not my fault you can't give people away as presents. "You look . . . did you fall?"

Andie looked down at her clothing as if she'd just realized what a mess she was. "Yeah, I did. I rode The Snake, and I was so dizzy when I got off, I lost my balance. Toppled right over, like an axed tree." She laughed. "But I wasn't the only one. Everyone else was staggering all over the place, too."

"You went on The Snake?" Eve frowned. "I thought you hated stuff like that." And besides, she thought to herself, I was just over there and The Snake wasn't running.

Andie shrugged. "Can't be a coward forever, right?" To Alfred, she said, "Where did you go, anyway? I followed you out of the food tent after Eve blew up at you, and you'd disappeared. Where were you?"

"Eve didn't 'blow up,'" Alfred corrected. "She was just upset, that's all. I don't blame her. And you must not have been looking very hard, because I was around." He waved a hand vaguely. "Just checking things out. A lot of people left after what happened to Boomer. We could probably close early if Eve wants."

"Eve doesn't want," Eve said. Closing early would be an admission that things weren't going well. She didn't want to admit that. "The signs along the highway say we're open until ten," she said firmly, "so we'll *be* open until ten. Besides," she added, sighing, "what else can happen? Don't you both think that's about it for today?"

Andie glanced up at the moon and joked, "You'd have to ask someone smarter than me. Like the man in the moon up there."

Eve followed Andie's gaze upward. The almost-full moon *was* pretty, she'd admit that. Well, not really pretty. More like . . . interesting, in a cold, distant way.

"Where's the rest of the committee?" she asked Andie, and got a shrug in reply.

"Who knows? Scattered all over the place, I guess. Let's hope one of them is making sure all of the darts in the dart booth are tipped with rubber suction cups."

"I already checked," Alfred said. "I checked every box. There wasn't a single metal tip in any of them."

Reassured, Eve decided to make the rounds one more time before the carnival closed. But this time, she took Andie and Alfred with her. If the threatening voice came again, she wanted someone else there to hear it, just to prove to herself that she wasn't losing her mind.

People *did* lose their minds from stress. From too much responsibility, too many hassles, too much flak. And the breakdown probably happened faster when the person with too much responsibility wasn't at all suited for it. If you put the wrong kind of engine in a car, it would break down. She was the wrong kind of engine for the Founders' Day celebration, so maybe she was already breaking down.

Someone *knew* that. Someone had guessed that Eve Forsythe was a phony, and was using that knowledge to hasten her breakdown.

That made Eve angry. Was someone trying to make her think she was hearing voices? Was that the idea? That stupid voice whispering about some silly "power," was she supposed to think she was imagining that? Well, she wasn't. And she knew she wasn't. The voice was really there, and it belonged to someone. Someone human, someone very real.

Who?

Even more puzzling was the question, *Why?*

"There you are!" Garth, with Serena, pink cotton candy in hand, beside him. "Don't tell me, let me guess, Andie. You rode The Snake. That's why you look such a mess."

Andie laughed. "You guessed it. Give that boy a prize! There should be a sign on that ticket booth that reads, RIDE AT YOUR OWN RISK."

"I've been on it four times already," Serena said dryly.

"Well, *you* live at Nightmare Hall," Andie retorted. "The Snake is probably tame in comparison."

"Gee, I'm sorry you feel that way, Andie," Serena said with a devilish grin, "because I was going to invite all of you over."

"Well, I just meant I wouldn't want to *live* there," Andie said. "It couldn't hurt to stop by just for a few minutes. I've been there before and came out in one piece."

When the committee gathered together at the exit at ten o'clock, Eve learned that of all of them, only she and Garth had never been inside Nightingale Hall. Even the townspeople on the committee had at one time or another visited the place.

Eve and the others on the campus committee climbed into Garth's car and headed for Vinnie's to pick up some pizza. Then they went on to Nightingale Hall.

Thanks to the brightness of the full moon, shining like a spotlight down on the house and grounds, the property didn't seem as ominous as usual when they pulled up the curving, gravel driveway.

Inside, Eve was impressed by the size of the house, with its high ceilings and spacious rooms, and its old, mellow woodwork. The library, with floor-to-ceiling shelves of books and a huge fireplace, seemed almost welcoming as Serena led them inside and placed the pizza boxes on a low, heavy wooden coffee table in the center of the room. The table was flanked by ugly brown upholstered furniture, but the long, narrow windows were open to the warm May breeze and silvery moonlight shone in on the worn Oriental carpet.

Serena took them on a tour of the three-story house. Eve was amazed to discover that she really liked it. In spite of its shabbiness, it seemed warmer and more welcoming, by far, than the immaculate but cold little house she'd grown up in.

"It's nicer than I expected," she admitted to Serena as they passed paper plates and napkins around. "But why did you pick this place instead of an on-campus dorm?"

"Money, pure and simple. I'm paying my own way through school and I watch my pennies carefully. I'd heard all the stories about this place before I'd even moved in. But it was cheap, and besides, I thought the stories were interesting. I keep waiting for a ghost or two to appear, but so far," Serena shrugged, "no luck."

"Too bad," Eve teased.

Serena shrugged. "I've always wanted to communicate with the other side."

"The other side?" Eve asked.

"Oh, you know," Serena said matter-of-factly, taking a slice of pizza and carefully sliding it onto her paper plate, "the other *side*. My parents are dead and there are a lot of things I didn't get to say while they were alive."

"You don't really believe that's possible, do you?" Eve asked.

"Who knows? But Dr. Litton says there are people who believe it's possible. You never know, right?"

Garth, pizza in hand, nodded. "True." Andie and Alfred nodded, too.

Eve felt like a square peg stuck in a round hole. Am I the only one? she wondered. Am I the only person in this room who has to see things to believe them? Maybe the voice was right tonight. Maybe I *do* have a narrow, closed little mind.

Once upon a time, she had had imagination. She had daydreamed, she had believed in leprechauns and the tooth fairy and Santa Claus, and she had believed that anything was possible. Anything.

But that was before she'd lived alone with Nell Forsythe for nine long, long, years.

Would she ever be who she used to be, who she really was?

Maybe it was too late.

Her hand reached up tentatively to the back of her head. She fingered the brass barrette. It would be so easy to unclasp it and set her hair free. Would that change anything? Would it free her mind as well as her hair?

Ridiculous. It wasn't as if she actually *wanted* to believe in the ability to speak to "the other side." And this wasn't the time for change. Not now. Not when she had so much to do.

That night when she and Andie got back to their room, Eve brushed her teeth, and flossed as usual. But she didn't hang up her blouse and skirt, just tossed them over a chair, ignoring the look of exaggerated shock on Andie's face and her wry commentary, "Am I really seeing what I think I'm seeing? Eve Forsythe not hanging up her clothes, which are color-coordinated in her closet? Maybe there's hope for you yet, roomie."

Too tired to take offense, Eve threw herself down on the bed.

And heard a whacking sound that she

shouldn't have heard when her head hit the pillow.

"Ow! What was *that*?" She sat up in bed, frowning.

"What was what?" Andie said, climbing into her own bed, on the opposite side of the room.

"That crack! There's something under my pillow." Eve reached over and turned the bedside lamp back on. Lifted her pillow. Saw a book. A hardcover book, small but wide. A children's book. One she was familiar with. Her mother had been too busy to read to her, but the children Eve had baby-sat for while she was in high school had two copies. It was their favorite book, and it hadn't taken her long to memorize it.

She reached down, lifted the book, held it up for Andie to see.

The title of the children's book, a popular one, the book that someone had hidden under her pillow, was *Moonchild*. It was the story of a sick, lonely little boy who, in his fantasies, had made friends with the man in the moon, and then went to live with him when he died.

Eve's eyes never left the cover. It was the drawing she was familiar with, had looked at countless times while baby-sitting. But there was something very wrong with the cover of this edition.

On the cover of the book she knew so well, a full, silvery moon had been clearly visible in a sky full of stars just outside the window of the child's hospital room.

The moon was still clearly visible on the cover she held in her hands. But there were two things wrong with it.

Someone had drawn, with black marker, a fat, dark cloud across the upper half of the round, silver orb.

But it was the lower half of the moon that held Eve's shocked gaze. It had been slashed with vivid streaks of bright red, dripping into the navy-blue night sky like . . .

Blood.

Chapter 13

"What *is* that?" Andie asked as Eve continued to sit quietly on the edge of her bed staring down at the book in her hands.

Mute, Eve held the book up so that Andie could see the cover.

"Oh, I know that book. My mother read it to me a couple of times when she was in a really good mood and felt like some mother-daughter bonding." Andie laughed harshly. "Which means, not very often." Then, "The cover looks different, though."

Eve found her voice. "It *is* different." She pointed out the two glaring violations.

"Oh, Eve, that's gross!" Andie got up and came over to examine the cover. "Are you sure it's supposed to be blood?" When she had studied the picture, she admitted, "It *does* look like it. I mean, the way it's dripping, what else could it be?" Leaving the book in Eve's hands, she returned to her own bed, sat on it with her knees drawn up and her arms encircling them. "That really is gross, Eve. It was under your pillow? How did it get there?"

A question Eve couldn't answer. With an index finger, she scraped absentmindedly at the dripping red. It remained in place. Marker. Indelible marker, she thought, just like the one I used in the Mirror Maze. Someone else on campus has discovered how useful markers can be.

"Eve," Andie said, her voice tense, "someone got in here while we were gone." She glanced around the room uneasily. "I don't like that. In fact, I *hate* it. If there's one thing I really get crazed about, it's my privacy. I made my father put a lock on my bedroom door when I was ten. Didn't we lock ours when we left?"

"I don't remember." Did it make any difference? If someone really wanted to get in to leave this disgusting . . . *thing* under her pillow, would a locked door have kept him out?

Eve glanced out the window. The moon, almost full, was still there, shining down upon campus.

"This," Eve said, waving the book and pulling her gaze away from the window to look at Andie, "has something to do with the moon." She hastily told Andie about the voice at The

Snake's ticket booth. When she repeated how the voice had scolded Eve for being 'contemptuous of the power of the moon,' " she desperately wanted Andie to laugh. She wanted Andie to point out how hilarious that was, how silly. If Andie would only dismiss it as nonsense, Eve could, too.

But Andie didn't do that. Instead, her green eyes opened wider and her freckles stood out in detail as her skin went white. "Eve! That's horrible! I thought maybe the book cover was just a stupid joke, but now . . . someone is *really* mad at you, Eve. Why didn't you tell me? Aren't you scared?"

Disappointed and unsettled by Andie's reaction, Eve snapped, "No, of course not! It's all just stupidity, that's why! Only an idiot would take it seriously." Liar, she thought. But she was so afraid that if she admitted her fear, it would become real. Then it would gain strength, become stronger than she. She'd fall apart. How could she fight back if she was in pieces, fragmented like the mirrors in the maze? "The power of the moon? Come *on*, Andie!"

Andie's flush told Eve that she, at least, would most certainly have taken the voice seriously. "Well, that's the second time today that you've called other people stupid," she said coldly, flopping down on her bed to lie on her back staring up at the ceiling. "You said practically the same thing to Alfred in the food tent. I don't blame him for getting mad, either."

"If only I could make Alfred stay mad at me."

Andie flipped over on her side, facing the wall, her back toward Eve. "If I were you, I'd take that message you found under your pillow seriously. It looks like some kind of warning to me. But then, you're *not* me, are you? You're not silly and stupid and gullible. You're . . . you're *logical*! Turn the light off, will you? I need to sleep, and it's not *logical* to try to sleep with the light on."

Eve knew she had been dismissed. Without ever getting any help or advice about the defaced book cover. She reached over and turned off the light, then she dropped the book on the floor and lay down in her bed. The moon cast silver stripes across the hardwood floor. They lay amid the clutter like an animal skin placed there to warm the feet on a cold winter night.

Eve lay on her side, staring at the moon-stripes. Andie was mad at her. And for what? For being "logical." Andie had made that seem almost as bad as being a serial killer.

How could you live in the world without being logical?

Eve reached down to pull the bedspread up

around her shoulders. If I believed in all that stuff in parapsychology class, she thought resentfully, I'd be terrified all the time. I don't *want* people using their minds to read mine, or to send objects flying across the room or set buildings on fire or cast spells. I don't want anyone in this world to have supernatural powers, not while I'm living in it. That is just *too* scary.

Of course none of it was true. None of it.

Then why was she so terrified? Why was her body trembling under the bedspread even though the temperature was a mild, balmy seventy degrees? Why were her fists clenched so tightly around the edge of the pillow? Why did her heart keep skipping a beat, and why did her feet feel like they were lying in a pool of ice water?

Because only the Eve she had become dismissed all of parapsychology as utter nonsense. Nell's perfectly logical daughter would never give a second thought to the idea of the moon having any kind of supernatural power. But the *other* Eve, the one who had created images in the clouds overhead as she lay under the grape arbor as a child, the one who had made up stories about every person who passed by on the street, the one who, when she read a book or saw a movie with an unhappy ending, had easily changed the ending in her own mind to a more satisfying one, *that* Eve was the person trembling in her bed in Lester dorm. That Eve still believed that all things, even weird ones, were possible.

No wonder my mother set out to change me, Eve thought in disgust. *This* Eve is a helpless, cowering wuss. No one would be able to stand her. *I* can't stand her! She certainly would never be elected to anything. She could sit for hours and daydream and draw and write stories and no one would care. No one would expect anything of her because they'd know she wasn't efficient or organized or responsible or . . . *logical* enough to deliver.

Her final thought before her eyes closed was: But if I *were* that other Eve, maybe no one would be smashing mirrors in my face and taunting me in the dark and leaving ugly messages under my pillow.

She fell asleep with her head tilted on the pillow, her face upturned toward the window and the silvery rays of the moon.

Chapter 14

Everyone's asleep now. I'm out here all alone, just me, so I can talk to you in private. I love being out here alone at night, with nothing but your bright light leading the way. It's so peaceful, so quiet, so private. I'd stay out here all night, but someone might catch me here and start asking questions.

Wasn't the book cover a stroke of genius? I hope Eve understood my message. It's hard, with narrow, closed minds like hers. Sometimes you just have to hammer them over the head to slip anything inside. Maybe my clever artwork was too subtle for her.

She can try to pass it off as a joke. But she can't fool me. The power sees right through her. I know she's really scared.

She'll tell the others. She'll show them the cover. She'll laugh and try to make fun of it, but I'll know what she's really feeling. And they're not as skeptical as she is. They'll see the warning for what it is. That will take care of any remaining doubt she might have about whether it's a serious message or not. They'll convince her.

I can't wait to see the terror in her eyes then.

There isn't another soul out here. Everyone's asleep. I think I'll just crawl into one of the Ferris wheel cars and sit there and think about what I'm going to do next. How best to use the power.

I'll have to try something else soon. Wouldn't want her, or any of the rest of them, to relax.

I love Ferris wheels. So big, so high off the ground, so dangerous, the way the cars swing and sway, especially at the very top. My mother hated them, would never go near one, and wouldn't let me, either. But I sneaked away from her and rode them, anyway. And after I used the power on her, I could ride anything I wanted, any time, any place.

Should have used it on her sooner.

Now, what shall I do next? Let me think . . .

Chapter 15

Andie wasn't in the room when Eve awoke to a gloomy Tuesday morning. The campus radio station announced that rain was expected later that day, and Eve thought grimly, Great! Perfect! Just what we need, a nice, drenching downpour, soaking the seats on the rides and turning the carnival grounds into a mucky mire. Perfect! If I believed in curses . . .

But she didn't, of course. Still, if she *did* believe in them, she would have been convinced that someone on campus was sticking pins into a doll that looked suspiciously like Eve Elizabeth Forsythe.

The book placed underneath her pillow the night before was still lying on the floor. Eve bent to pick it up. She should show it to someone. But who? The police wouldn't take it seriously. The committee? Maybe. Alfred wouldn't laugh. He wouldn't think it was funny, or harmless. He was already worried about her, wanted to protect her, keep her safe.

Well, she would keep *herself* safe, thank you very much. Alfred wasn't going to become her self-appointed bodyguard.

She had just tossed the book into the wastebasket when Andie arrived, saying grimly, "Get dressed. Fast. The dean wants to see you. Us. The committee. I think it's about Boomer. What are we going to tell her? I mean, we don't know *where* that dart came from."

Eve's stomach had already been queasy because of the book cover. Now, it somersaulted. What were they going to say to the dean? She would have questions. She would want answers. A popular Salem University athlete was in the hospital, and no one on the committee had any idea how that had happened.

There was no time to confer with the rest of the committee, so, when they were all standing, nervous and uncertain, in the dean's office, Eve told the simple truth. "We don't know how that dart got there," she admitted. "And we don't know who threw it, or why." There. She had just confessed that she didn't know what was going on at the carnival she was supposed to be in charge of. Maybe now the dean would fire her. Relieve her of her duties. Assign someone more capable and trustworthy to take over.

But when they left the office a few minutes later, Eve was still cochairperson of the Founders' Day celebration committee.

"The police believe that what happened yesterday was an accident," the dean had said. "It looks like that one dart became mixed in with the others during packing. The company will be held responsible for Boomer's medical bills, and his parents seem satisfied with that. Just to be on the safe side, however, we have employed additional security personnel for the duration of the festivities. All I ask on your part is that you check everything out very carefully before the carnival opens each day. There cannot possibly be a repeat of yesterday's disaster at any of the game booths."

At no time had she said, "And Eve, since you haven't been doing a very good job, I've decided to replace you. I'm sure you can understand why."

Eve's emotions were so mixed when she left the office that she couldn't be sure which feeling was stronger: disappointment or relief. Besides, one question hadn't been answered. Even if the metal-tipped dart had accidentally been packed in their box, *who* had thrown it?

Tony hadn't. Wasn't that the most important question of all?

"The dean is really behind us," Serena commented as they left the building, emerging into a chilly, gray day. "I mean, she could have canceled the whole thing. I'll bet the board was pressuring her to."

"Nah," Alfred disagreed. "It was probably the other way around. The board wants the money we're going to bring in. They'll keep this thing going as long as they can, no matter what happens."

Eve didn't like the sound of that. "You make it sound as if you expect more trouble. Please don't even hint at that, Alfred. Things are bad enough already."

Alfred looked up at the dismally gray sky. "Well, sorry, Eve, but I think our problem *du jour* is going to be nasty weather. I think the only sound we're going to hear coming from the cash registers tonight is the plink-plink of rain hitting the keys."

He was right. The skies opened before noon and by the time Eve left her last class, shortly after one o'clock, and went to the carnival site to check things out, the ground was a sloppy mess, the seats on every ride were thoroughly sodden, the canvas tent, shielding the food, sagging around its tent poles. The rain showed no sign of letting up. The sky was a thick, depressing slate-gray all the way to the horizon.

Eve conferred with every member of the committee by telephone, and they all agreed. There would be no carnival that day.

Eve notified the campus and local radio stations. She enlisted Andie's and Serena's aid in driving along the highway to post CLOSED DUE TO WEATHER signs on top of the original carnival signs. They hung another, larger one on the entrance to the site.

"What a drag!" Serena complained as they drove to Nightmare Hall to drop her off. "Now what are we going to do tonight?"

"Study for finals!" Andie answered without hesitation. "That's why I wanted the carnival held earlier in the month. We're doing double-duty here, getting ready for finals and handling the Founders' Day stuff. I'm behind in two term papers and haven't even opened a book for my chem final. As far as I'm concerned, this rain is a gift from heaven."

"I didn't know you wanted the carnival held earlier," Eve said as Serena climbed out of the car. Nightmare Hall looked gloomier than ever, black sky behind it, a thick curtain of rain surrounding it. "You never said anything."

Andie shrugged. "Everyone else was pushing for this week, especially Kevin. Alfred and

Serena were, too. Kevin being cochairperson, I figured he'd get what he wanted. Anyway, I was outvoted, so why make a fuss?"

Serena waved and ran through the rain to the front porch, where she waved again before going inside.

"Whew," Andie said as Eve drove down the gravel driveway, "how'd you like to go home to that place on such a gloomy day?"

Eve laughed. "I wouldn't want to go home to that place even on a sunny day. Although it's not as bad inside as I thought it would be." And, she thought to herself, it's not as if I feel so incredibly safe at Lester right now, not after I found that book under my pillow.

When they got back to their room, they went downstairs to the dining hall for a quick meal. Then Andie, books piled high on her bed, settled in for a long evening of studying.

"I'm going to do that, too," Eve said, slipping into a red slicker with a matching, floppy-brimmed hat, and pulling on an old pair of sneakers. "But first, I want to check things out at the site."

Andie lifted her head. "You're going over to the carnival? Now? In this weather?"

Eve frowned. "You sound like my mother. Well, not *my* mother. Weather never stopped her from doing anything. But you sound like *someone*'s mother. I'm just going to check things out, make sure the food tent didn't collapse under all that water, stuff like that. I'll be right back." The truth was, she had a funny feeling. She couldn't have explained it to Andie, wasn't even going to try. But every time she thought about the site, her spine crawled, and she had a creepy feeling that meant something. There could be something wrong over there.

There was doubt in Andie's face. She hesitated for a second, then said, "Eve? Do you really think you should go alone? If you really have to go over there, why don't you call Alfred, or that guy, Garth, see if one of them will go with you."

Pretending she wasn't worried, Eve said testily, "Now you really *do* sound like someone's mother. No one is even going to be at that site, Andie. Who besides me is dumb enough to go out in this? The place will be totally deserted. I'll be as safe as I would be in my own bed."

Andie's head bent over her books. "Yeah," she muttered, "but just remember someone *put* something in that bed last night. I rest my case."

Good point. "Well, you'll be happy to know I'm taking a flashlight, Mom. See you."

Andie didn't answer as Eve left the room.

It's all an act, Eve thought as she hurried down the hall, her sneakers making a whispering sound on the hardwood floor. The dorm was quiet with the hush of people studying. I really don't want to go anywhere near the carnival. It'll be dark, and filthy with mud, and it's raining so hard, I won't be able to see anything. If there really is something wrong, can't it wait until morning? What am I trying to prove, anyway?

That you're not afraid, her brain answered.

Then why am I examining the elevator so carefully before I step inside? Eve argued half-seriously.

The carnival site was even more depressing than she'd expected. Without the lights from the Ferris wheel and the other rides, and the moon completely hidden somewhere in the charcoal sky, only the narrow beam of Eve's flashlight broke the darkness. She was forced to keep the light aimed downward to trace the safest path through deep puddles and treacherous mud. Even so, she slipped and slid as if she were walking across a glassy frozen pond.

She had never heard such quiet. No music, no laughter, no chatter, no balloons popping, no crack of air rifles targetting marching ducks, no shrieks and screams coming from the rides. Occasionally, a car high at the top of the Ferris wheel would creak as a sudden gust of wind caught it and sent it swinging. But there were no other sounds.

She missed the smells, too, of popcorn and hot dogs and the sugary-sweet smell of cotton candy. The food booths were draped completely with black, heavy canvas. The silent, dripping boxlike shapes loomed up out of the darkness on both sides of Eve, as if they were watching, waiting to see what she would do, why she was there.

Why *am* I here? she wondered as a gust of wind slapped her in the face with a sheet of rain so cold, it took her breath away. Andie was right. This is stupid. No one else is dumb enough to come out in this kind of weather. I haven't proved a single thing to anyone except that, at least, the carnival site is still intact. Soaked and dismal, but intact. No one blew it up or set fire to it.

Maybe now that clammy feeling in her spine would disappear and she could concentrate on studying for finals.

Keeping her flashlight aimed on the muddy ground ahead of her, Eve turned and was about to head back to the dorm, when the total silence was broken by the sound of a voice.

"Ee-vie! Oh, Ee-vie, where you going? Leaving so soon? But you just got here!"

Chapter 16

At the sound of the sickeningly familiar whisper, Eve froze. The mud in which she was standing ankle-deep might as well have been quick-drying cement. After several minutes of silence broken only by the creaking of the Ferris wheel and the slapping of rain onto canvas, she lifted her head away from the path drawn by her flashlight. Her eyes darted from side to side, but her legs remained immobile.

"Ee-vie? Nice weather, huh? So how come you're out here? I wouldn't have figured you for one of those too-dumb-to-come-in-out-of-the-rain people. I thought you were smarter than that. I can't believe they put someone so stupid in charge of the Founders' Day committee."

Mute and miserable, with water dripping steadily from the brim of her hat, Eve remained rooted to the spot. Andie's earlier question sprang into her mind. "Shouldn't you take someone with you?" The answer to that question was yes. A big, fat, rotten yes.

Too late now.

What was it she was supposed to be proving out here? Oh, yes, that she wasn't afraid.

"Where are you?" she called, peering anxiously through the rain curtain. When no answer came, she cleared her throat and repeated the question, louder this time. "Where *are* you?"

"Wouldn't you like to know? Maybe I'm not anywhere. Maybe I'm everywhere."

Eve wouldn't argue that. It certainly seemed that way to her.

Her legs finally agreed to move, and she began tentatively backing up, yanking first one foot out of the mud, then the other. If she couldn't see who was there because of the rain, maybe they couldn't see her too well, either. It was the only hope she had.

That hope died instantly when the voice said, *"And just where do we think we're going? Where are your manners, Eve? I haven't dismissed you."*

Eve whirled and began to run. *Tried* to run. Slogging through mud couldn't be called running, and the wind and the rain were against her. She felt like one of the street mimes she'd seen in San Francisco, pushing against an invisible wall.

As she slogged, her head swiveled from side to side under her hood. Where could she go? Was there someplace safe to hide, until the voice went away? *Would* it go away? Or was it, this time, determined to finish the job it had started in the Mirror Maze?

She couldn't move quickly, but her mind was racing. Where to hide? Where to find safety? To get back to the dorm, she'd have to run out into the open, giving him a perfect, unprotected target. It was too far, and too dangerous.

The Ferris wheel? Could she hide in one of the seats? No. The red raincoat would be too visible. The Snake? That ride was so dangerous that the front of the wooden seats rose high, to chest level, providing some protection for the rider. And . . . maybe . . . if she could make it that far, climb in and slide down in one of the seats behind the wooden shield. . . . She could hide in the seat until she was sure he'd given up and left the carnival grounds. Then she'd make a break for the dorm and safety.

If she could just get to The Snake without being seen.

She slid sideways on the muddy grass, into the shadow of the booths, moving in and out among them stealthily, like a thief in the night.

"*Ee-vie! Where are you? I can't have this, you know. You keep disappearing on me. That's so rude.*"

Good. If he wasn't lying, trying to trick her, he couldn't see her now. If she stuck closely to the booths, maybe the shadows would protect her until she reached The Snake.

She slipped and fell twice. The first time, her hat fell off and skidded away. Terrified that he would pounce on her while she was lying helpless in the mud, Eve struggled to her feet and ran, leaving the hat behind. The second time, she lost the flashlight. That was far more serious than losing the hat, and she wasted precious moments fumbling around in the mud with her hands. But the bulb had gone out when the flashlight landed. Trying to find it in the dark would take too long.

"*Oh, Ee-vie! Where are you?*" the voice sing-songed from a distance.

The sound chilled Eve's blood. But it *was* from a distance, which meant she still had time. Only minutes, maybe seconds, but she was grateful for that much.

She could see The Snake through the rain now. It lay coiled and silent on its tracks. Hope rose in her throat. It did seem from this distance as if someone lying curled up on one of the seats would be completely hidden behind the high wooden front. She'd be safe there. Until he gave up and left.

"*Eve!*" Angry now, that voice. "*Where are you? You really are stupid, making me angry. My own mother made me angry, and I killed her. I killed my own mother, Evie! Anger fuels my power. You're just making me stronger. That's a really big mistake.*"

Power, schmower, Eve thought in disgust, climbing under the rope that barred the entrance to The Snake. You're a head case, that's all you are. But a dangerous one, I'll give you that.

Eve's barrette was long gone, and her sodden hair clung to her cheeks, dripping rainwater into her eyes. She had to continually brush it aside to see.

There! That last car, at the very end. Its wooden front, decorated with a wicked-looking snake, fangs exposed, painted in bright reds and greens, looked higher than the others. If she could just make it along the wooden platform without being seen, she'd be well hidden in there.

Terrified that she might be spotted, Eve fell to her hands and knees and crawled along the platform, the cold rain pelting down upon her. The surface was slick, and she had to go slowly, for fear of sliding off the edge and landing on the ground underneath the ride.

Where were all those extra security guards the dean had promised? she wondered bitterly as she finally reached the last car. Why was she all alone out here?

"Ee-vie! I'm right behind you!"

Well, not really *alone*.

Carefully, struggling to stay as low as possible, Eve grabbed the handles on the last car of The Snake and pulled herself up onto its floor. She lay there, breathing erratically for several minutes before moving up to the seat, where she rolled herself into a tight little ball, knees drawn up, head lowered into her chest. It was wet and cold and uncomfortable. But, hidden behind the wooden shield, she felt a little safer than she had since she'd first heard the voice.

Silence. All around her. The wind hissed and the rain splashed down upon the seat and the platform and pinged loudly on her red slicker, but no oily, evil voice purred in her ear.

How would she know he had given up? How could she be sure? Even if she dared to sit up and look, she wouldn't be able to see more than a few feet in front of her, because of the downpour. Better to stay quiet and hidden for as long as she could bear it.

Not too long ago, while she was looking for a birthday card for Andie, she had come across a get-well card that read, "Misery is lying in bed with a cold and an empty box of tissues."

Wrong. Misery, she knew now, was lying scrunched-up on a hard, cold, puddled wooden seat in the middle of a rainstorm hiding from a maniac who is ranting and raving about some weird "power" and won't rest until you're stone-cold dead, and you don't have a clue about why any of it is happening. That, it seemed to Eve, was true misery.

Lost in that misery, she didn't realize at first that a new noise had joined the hissing of the wind. This one was louder, a creaking groan that began slowly and then quickly rose to a grinding, whirring noise, like when she'd tried to learn to drive a standard transmission car and had almost stripped the gears.

Not moving a muscle, Eve strained to listen more carefully.

But before she could place the sound, the car in which she had sought refuge lurched forward.

The Snake was moving!

Letting out a small, frightened cry, Eve bolted upright.

The Snake gathered speed so quickly, there was no time to jump free, even if she hadn't been too frozen with terror to move. Although its lights never came on and its music never began playing, in the space of less than a minute, her "refuge" became a racing prison, whipping back and forth so quickly and at such impossible angles that, after only a second or two, Eve's neck felt as if it were about to snap in two and send her head flying out into space.

There was no time to grasp the black safety belt and fasten it around her chest and shoulders. It sat, unused, flapping uselessly against the back of the seat.

Crying silently, "No, no, this can't be happening!" Eve's hand flew out instead to grasp the metal rail stationed across the wooden shield in front of her. She held on with all of her strength, and still her body was flung back and forth like a tennis ball as The Snake raced along its serpentine tracks. On the sharpest, most abrupt angles, Eve was lifted bodily off the seat. Had she not had the railing to cling to, she would have been flung free.

She hung on desperately. The wind, sharpened by the speed of the ride, forced her eyes closed. Her shoulders were on fire. Her chest heaved in an effort to catch her breath as the wicked ride zigzagged sharply left, then right, then back again, without warning.

Just when she knew she couldn't hang on

another second, The Snake suddenly slowed and came to a halt.

Eve sobbed with relief.

But she was completely drained, her knees nothing but sawdust, and before she could straighten up and tumble free of the car onto the platform, the grinding sound came again and The Snake took off a second time.

"Oh, God, no!" Eve screamed into the wind and the rain, "No!" but in vain. She was already speeding around yet another hairpin curve, her head snapping like a whip being cracked.

There'd be no getting off until the death-defying cycle had been repeated.

Eve struggled to think. The ride had to be on a timer. Which meant it would stop periodically. But the person handling the controls out here in the dark and the rain had no intention of letting her off. His goal was clear: to keep her on this thing until she was too exhausted to hold onto the railing any longer. Then The Snake would whip around one of the deadlier curves and her body would be tossed like a Frisbee, up into the air and out into the cold, wet night.

There was only one way to save herself.

She had to get off this ride.

And she had to get off it *before* it slowed to

a stop. That pause would only last a second, and he'd be watching her, making sure she didn't pull herself together enough to jump free.

She would have to get off while The Snake was still moving. And she would have to do it when her car was on the far side of the ride, away from the controls, where he had to be stationed. If she could work up the courage to jump, and time it just right . . . the jump to the ground wasn't that great a distance. Maybe no bones would be broken. Maybe . . . maybe she'd even be able to get up and run, before he realized the car was empty.

The Snake was going so *fast!* If she jumped from a car going this fast, only a miracle would save her. But she couldn't hang on much longer.

Heads I lose, tails I don't win, she told herself grimly as the car whipped back and forth, back and forth, making her dizzy, tugging fiercely on her shoulders as her hands continued to grip the metal bar.

The rain was pelting down even harder, and it was hard to tell exactly where on the tracks she was now. The far side, away from the controls? There, off to her left in the distance, she could make out a large building — it had to be the top of the administration building. That meant . . . that meant that they were just about to whiz around the last, nasty curve before plunging into the section she felt would give her the best chance of jumping unseen.

Still clutching the rail, Eve sat up very straight. She leaned over the side of the car, hoping to see something, anything, that would give her hope. She saw nothing but a thick wall of rain.

If she jumped at the wrong moment, if she picked the wrong spot, if she landed the wrong way . . .

"Oh, God, I can't do this," she cried aloud. "This is insane! It's too fast, I'm off-balance, I'm too tired . . ."

"Hey, Ee-vie!"

She could barely hear the voice above the roar of the ride.

"Ee-vie, isn't this a blast? I hope you're holding on. Are you holding on, Evie? Pretty soon, you'll be too tired to hold on, you know. Then the power will lift you right up and out of that seat, and you'll take flight. Probably always wanted to fly, right, Evie? Wild, loud laughter.

Eve stood up, leaned as far over the side of the car as she dared, and jumped.

Chapter 17

"Eve? Eve, are you awake?"

Eve opened her eyes to find herself lying in her own bed. The red slicker was gone, and her wet clothes had been removed. She was wrapped in her white terrycloth robe. It was warm and dry, as were the blankets covering her legs. Andie, her own hair curling with dampness, a towel slung over her shoulders, stood at the foot of Eve's bed.

She must have just taken a shower, Eve thought, her eyelids heavy. Did I take one, too? I don't remember, but my hair is wet, like Andie's.

Garth was standing right behind Andie. His hair, too, was damp, plastered against his forehead in dark, wavy strands.

Eve struggled awake. Why was everybody's hair wet? And what was Garth doing in her room?

"He found you," Andie said, reading the expression on Eve's face. "Garth found you, lying on the ground near The Snake." She sat down on the edge of Eve's bed. "He came here looking for you, a little while ago, and I told him you'd gone to the carnival site." She smiled up at Garth gratefully. "Thank goodness he went looking for you. And he found you."

"You were totally out of it," Garth said, dropping into Eve's desk chair. "I almost didn't spot you. The rain made it hard to see, and you weren't making a sound. I would have walked right by you if you hadn't been wearing red. That helped."

Eve raised herself up on her elbows. Her head swam and a wave of dizziness sent her flat on the pillow again, her damp hair splaying out around her.

"Eve," Andie said flatly, "what in God's name were you doing at that awful ride?" When Eve didn't answer, she continued, "Maybe you should go to the infirmary. Are you okay?"

Eve reached up and fingered the bump on her forehead. Her vision wasn't blurring and she didn't seem to have any broken bones. "I don't need to go to the infirmary. I'm fine."

"Garth said it looked to him like you'd fallen off The Snake." Andie frowned. "But the carnival is closed and none of the rides are operating, so we knew that didn't make any sense."

"I didn't fall out," Eve said wearily. She wished they would both go away. All she wanted to do was sleep. "I jumped. And The Snake *was* running. I was hiding in the last car, trying to get away from the voice, when someone started it up. The ride, I mean. And then they wouldn't stop it long enough for me to jump out. So I had to jump out when it was still moving. There wasn't any other choice."

A flurry of questions tumbled out of both of them. Eve had a bad headache and she couldn't think and she couldn't answer the questions, anyway, because she didn't know anything. She remembered the terrible feeling of panic when she was in that car and she remembered jumping and she even remembered hitting the ground and how much that had hurt, and she remembered feeling relieved that she wasn't dead because she felt the chill from the deep puddle of water she had landed in, which had probably cushioned her fall. Her last thought before she lost consciousness had been, I could probably drown in this puddle.

She remembered nothing after that. She didn't remember Garth finding her or being carried back to the dorm room or Andie's removing her wet clothes.

But she remembered, too well, the terror of

being on that ride and the desperate need to get away from it.

"I need to sleep," she said, and rolled over on her side. She was asleep in seconds.

The next morning, Garth called to make sure Eve was okay. She had only one question for him. "Did you see anyone?" she asked anxiously, ignoring her throbbing headache and the agonizing pain in both shoulders, the aching bruises on her arms and legs. The sun streaming in through the window hurt her eyes. "When you found me, was anyone else there?"

"Nope. Only you. Why?"

"Because I didn't jump from that car for exercise," Eve snapped. "I *told* you, I heard that voice again. The same one I heard in the Mirror Maze. It was after me. It called me by name. Are you sure you didn't see anything?"

"Not a thing. But it was raining like crazy, Eve. I almost didn't see *you*, and I was *looking* for you. I wasn't looking for anyone else." Garth paused, then added, "I saw Alfred and Serena, but that was later, after I brought you back. I went downstairs to get hot coffee for Andie and me, and Alfred was at the vending machine. Serena was right behind him. They looked like drowned rats."

"Did you tell them what happened?"

"No. Wasn't sure you'd want me to."

"Serena lives at Nightmare Hall. I wonder what she was doing on campus so late."

"Said she'd been hitting the books at the library. Studying for finals. And good old Alfred wanted to know what *I* was doing in your building."

"What did you tell him?"

"I said we were studying, together. He didn't like it, gave me one of those looks. Are you going to tell them what happened? Shouldn't they know? Seems to me everyone you know should be on the alert. Keeping an eye out. Unless you're planning on closing down the festivities now."

Close down the Founders' Day celebration? Now? Wouldn't that be a huge relief? Like having a ten-ton boulder lifted off the back of her neck. Everything horrible that had happened this week had to be connected to the celebration, although Eve couldn't think of a single reason why that would be true. If the carnival ended, would the other stuff end, too? Would she be safe, then? Would they all be safe?

"No," she said firmly, in spite of her aches and pains and the leftover terror still chilling her spine, "we're not closing down."

"No?" He sounded surprised, but he didn't argue, and shortly afterward, they hung up.

Eve thought about calling the police. But she had no proof. Nothing at all. Her pursuer wasn't stupid. There wouldn't be any finger-prints on The Snake's operating lever. And the rain would have washed away any footprints. She had nothing.

But she *would* be more careful from now on.

If she only knew *why* . . . maybe that would help. The gibberish the voice had spouted, about the moon and some stupid "power," pro-vided no information at all. Only someone to-tally insane would do the things he was doing, and rant and rave about weird, impossible things.

Dealing with someone who was out of his mind was a lot scarier than dealing with some-one simply angry, for whatever reason, about the Founders' Day festivities.

Why hadn't he killed her last night when she was lying unconscious in that puddle? What had stopped him? Maybe Garth had come along too soon and spoiled everything by finding Eve first.

It took Eve a long time in parapsychology class to work up enough nerve to ask the ques-tion that was making her crazy. She knew everyone would stare when she opened her mouth. She'd made her scorn for the paranor-mal obvious from the very first day of class.

Now they'd think she'd converted, that she was becoming a believer.

Never. But she *had* to ask this question.

"Dr. Litton," she said, clenching her fist around a pencil, keeping her voice clear and steady, "*can* the full moon make people do things they wouldn't normally do?"

Heads swiveled and there were suddenly so many eyes on Eve, she felt like an exhibit at the zoo. Andie's mouth had fallen open, and Eve saw Alfred and Serena exchange a glance of total disbelief.

Eve felt the blood rush to her face. For pete's sake, she hadn't asked if there really was a man in the moon.

The professor seemed to take the question seriously. "I think the answer to that, Ms. Forsythe, is that if someone *believed* the moon at its fullest was affecting his or her behavior, truly believed it, then yes, the behavior would undoubtedly change. Literature is filled with references to such behavior, as we've already discussed in here."

Eve was pleased with Dr. Litton's answer. And before anyone could argue with it, the bell rang. Eve put her notebook into her backpack, as people grabbed their books and jumped up, heading for the door.

Eve slid her feet back inside her black flats

and would have stood up, too. But just then her fingers closed around something inside the backpack that shouldn't have been there. Something *she* hadn't put there. In fact, something that she had tossed into the wastebasket because she couldn't bear the sight of it.

The room emptied quickly, but still Eve sat, her eyes staring straight ahead as her hand pulled from the backpack the hardcover copy of *Moonchild*.

She knew that's what it was, although she didn't look down at first. She didn't want to look down. She could tell by the feel of it, by the shape of it, and by the feeling deep inside her stomach.

She *wouldn't* look down. She would simply stand up, walk to the huge gray metal trash can beside Dr. Litton's desk, toss the book in, and leave the room. One, two, three, easy as pie. No problem.

She looked down.

The book sat in her lap, cover up. The moon was there, visible from the child's hospital room. The shadow was still painted across the upper half, and the lower half was still red with "blood."

But now there was more. The vicious artist had drawn a "mouth" on the moon. Not a smiley mouth. Definitely not a smiley mouth, Eve thought, sickened, her eyes fixated on the crude, horrifying drawing.

Instead of a pleasant smile on the moon, there was a wide, maniacal grin filled with pointed, razor-sharp teeth.

Chapter 18

The next thing Eve knew, she was lying on the floor, staring up at Serena and Dr. Litton.

"Should we call a doctor?" the professor asked.

"You fainted," Serena told Eve. There was awe in her voice.

"I know, I know," Eve said, sitting up and leaning against the professor's desk, "I'm not the type. Should have eaten more than a bagel, I guess." She didn't want them to know about the book, but they'd probably already seen it. How was she going to explain it?

"Are you sure that's all it is?" Dr. Litton asked. "You were only out for a second, but people don't faint without a reason."

Oh, I had a reason, Eve thought darkly. She glanced around her, looking for the book. It had probably fallen to the floor when she slid out of her seat. "There was a book . . ." she began, but Serena interrupted her.

"That horrible thing? I saw it. It was disgusting. Is that why you passed out? I tossed it down the incinerator chute. I didn't want you seeing it when you woke up. I hope that's okay. I mean, you didn't *want* it, did you, Eve?"

Dr. Litton nodded. "I saw it, too. Who drew on the cover?"

"I don't know," Eve said.

"I would suggest that you go back to your room and take the morning off," Dr. Litton said, helping Eve up. "You've got a nasty bruise on your forehead. Did that happen just now?"

Eve almost laughed. Which disaster was the bruise from? It was hard to keep track these days. "No," was all she said.

Serena went with her to Lester. On the way, she said, "I don't blame you for folding like an accordion. Are you sure you're okay?"

"I will be." Eve was trying to think when that book might have been placed in her backpack. The only time she remembered putting the pack down was when she had grabbed a quick cup of coffee and a bagel that morning before class. She'd left the backpack on her chair when she went to get sugar. But she'd only been gone a second. And she hadn't noticed anyone skulking around her chair.

What scared her the most was the realization that the sick "artist" who had thrust that book into her backpack had been *close* to her. And she hadn't even known it.

Andie wasn't in the room when they went inside.

"You're going to stay here, right?" Serena asked anxiously. "I mean, if I leave, you're not going to get up and go to classes, are you? You need to rest."

When Eve sat down on the bed, a wave of dizziness so strong it blurred her vision slapped at her. She swayed precariously. Serena reached over and gently helped her lie down.

"You shouldn't have gotten out of bed this morning. Andie told me what happened last night. I have a mythology class, but I've already read all of the material, so I can stay if you want. I hate leaving you here all alone."

"I'm just going to sleep, Serena. Go ahead and go. I can't sleep with someone staring at me, anyway. But I'll be at the carnival grounds at two, for sure."

"Oh, you don't have to go over there, Eve. Kevin's being sprung this morning. Didn't anyone tell you? He's fine, and he'll be there. You've been doing double-duty long enough. Let him take over now."

Eve sighed with relief. Kevin was back. She

wasn't alone anymore. The truth was, it felt wonderful to lie down and close her eyes. Shut everything out. She would burrow deep beneath the blankets and pretend that she was safe.

"Okay, I'll stay here," she said meekly, rolling over on her side. Serena pulled the bedspread over her. "For a little while. I guess I *am* tired."

Serena closed the door quietly when she left.

Eve concentrated on shutting out the horrible image of bloody moon fangs, and fell asleep.

When she awoke, the clock on her bedside table said two-twenty. Eve couldn't believe it. She had slept for over three hours! The carnival had already opened, and here she was, lying in bed like a sloth. Nell would have a screaming fit if she knew her responsible, levelheaded daughter was sleeping off her duties like some garden slug.

Then she remembered that Kevin was back, and she sagged back against the pillow. She didn't have to get up. She didn't have to do anything. Kevin could do it all. Serena was right, she *had* been doing "double-duty" while Kevin's ribs were healing. It was his turn.

But . . . Eve struggled to force her mind fully awake . . . weren't there other things she needed to attend to? Kevin could handle things at the carnival site. But he couldn't find out why that book had been in her backpack or why Boomer had been shot with that dart or who had put that burr under the horse's saddle, starting the whole, nasty business.

Neither can I, she thought as she sat up gingerly, waiting for another wave of dizziness. It didn't come, and she swung her feet to the floor. I'm no detective. The police are supposed to be looking for the person who put a hole in Boomer's chest.

But there was something she could do. She could go see Boomer herself. Ask him straight out, if he had seen anything. Seen *anyone*. If he had seen who threw the dart, that made him an eyewitness. An eyewitness was even better than fingerprints, wasn't it?

You're not being very realistic, she told herself as she changed out of her wrinkled clothes into clean cutoffs and a red tank top. Where's that marvelous logic people keep talking about? The police must have asked Boomer what he'd seen. If he'd given them a name, the guilty party would have been arrested by now.

Clinging to a faint hope that the police simply hadn't had time yet to talk to Boomer, Eve left the dorm and climbed on the little yellow shuttle bus into town. She couldn't shake the feeling that she had to do *something*, and that she had to do it *fast*. Someone had been in her room. Someone had grabbed that book out of the wastebasket, and that same someone had then slid it into her backpack. Knowing that made her palms sweaty and the hair on the back of her neck stand on end. So close . . . he had been so *close*. And she hadn't even known it!

Talking to Boomer, even if the conversation was futile, was better than lying in bed terrified, with her heart threatening to pound its way right out of her chest.

The nurse on the fourth floor at the Twin Falls Medical Center gave her a hard time. "He's still in serious condition. If you're not a relative . . ."

"I'm his cousin," Eve said quickly. Ignoring the skeptical eyebrow lifting toward the nurse's cap, she added, "We're very close. That's why we decided to go to the same college."

"Funny," the nurse said drily, "his parents have been here for two days and they never mentioned a cousin." But she relented, and waved Eve toward Boomer's room.

Boomer's face was waxy white, his eyes still puzzled because he had no idea how someone as big and healthy as he was could have ended up flat on his back in a hospital bed. He was so glad to have company that Eve didn't have the heart to ask him any questions about the dart. She made lively conversation until it was time for her to leave. Finally she had to say as matter-of-factly as she could, "Boomer, I was just wondering if you saw who threw that dart at you. I mean, you were facing the crowd. I figured you might have seen an arm raised or something."

"Just Tony's arm," was his disappointing answer. "I was pretty much keeping my eyes on Tony. He'd already hit the apple with every dart he'd thrown, so I was trying to figure out a way to maybe duck or something, move a little bit to one side just so the last dart would miss. Take him down a peg or two. But then I decided that wouldn't be fair, so I stood still."

Eve was crushed. Boomer had been her only hope. "You didn't see anything? Someone watching you from the crowd, looking like they were waving?" They hadn't been waving, of course. They'd been aiming. But she didn't want to say that.

Boomer thought for a minute, his lips pursed, his brow furrowed in concentration. "I knew everyone in the crowd. The ones near the back were on your carnival committee, pretty much. Well, except for one guy — the guy from the camera shop? He kind of waved a little, but

·I didn't think he was waving at me."

Garth? Eve thought as she walked down the quiet hallway toward the elevator. No wonder he'd appeared on the scene right away, warning her not to remove the dart. He'd been right there the whole time. If she hadn't gone around to the back of the booth, she'd have seen him.

She stabbed the down button, waited for the elevator to arrive. It wasn't as if Garth had been the only person watching Tony throw. There'd been a huge crowd.

Garth wouldn't hurt anyone, Eve thought vehemently as she stepped into the elevator.

How do *you* know? a little voice asked her. You just met him. Don't forget, he has good reason to be mad at the administration. Reason enough to get back at the dean and the board of trustees by ruining the Founders' Day celebration. True, he didn't seem angry, but that could all be just an act. You don't know what's going on in his head.

Boomer had thought Garth was waving at him. Why would Garth have been waving at him?

Eve's head began to ache again.

Chapter 19

Garth was waiting for Eve near the Ferris wheel. He looked angry. His mouth was a thin line, and his thick, dark eyebrows met in a scowl. "I can't believe you're out here," he said, moving toward Eve. She saw Serena at the cotton candy booth, Kevin near the Ferris wheel, and Alfred was waving to her from the dart booth. Checking the darts again, no doubt. Good thinking.

"Why wouldn't I be out here?" she said flippantly, glancing around her, trying to make the glance look casual. Everything seemed . . . normal. The carnival had been open for a couple of hours now, and there was a large crowd. If she concentrated really hard, she could pretend that everything *was* normal. "I'm cochairperson of an event. This," waving her hands to encompass her surroundings, "is the event. So where else should I be?"

"In your room, in your bed!" he barked, taking her elbow and leading her into the shelter of the Ferris wheel. "After last night, and then what happened this morning . . . Serena filled me in . . . I was sure you'd resign. Or sign yourself into the infirmary. This whole damn thing should have been canceled. Your administration is out to lunch, if you ask me. And you, what are *you* trying to prove? You're smart enough to know you could have been killed on that ride last night."

"Well, thank you so much for reminding me. Just the thing to brighten my day. Have you ever thought of writing greeting cards for a living?" The little men hammering inside her skull stepped up their pace. "And speaking of earning a living, why aren't you at work? You sure take a lot of time off." If he went back to town, she wouldn't have to see him, wouldn't have to look at him and wonder.

His scowl deepened. "What's the matter with you? I'm here because I was worried. I went back to your room, and you weren't there. Came here, found Andie, and she said she'd bet anything you were out here somewhere. She was right, wasn't she? I can't believe it. Call me crazy, but it seems to me that someone tried to stop your clock last night. Generous of you to give them a second chance. You like being a target, is that it?"

She had never seen him so angry. He seemed like a completely different person.

"I am *not* hiding in my room like a fugitive," she said hotly. "My mistake was in coming here alone last night." She waved her hands at the crowd. "I'm not alone now, am I? And I won't be for the rest of the day. So what's the big deal?" .

Behind them, the Ferris wheel began revolving slowly, its music a loud, perky tune. Eve glanced up at it, thinking how tiny they must look to the people in the car at the very top. It was swaying gently, and she could see arms waving. "You thought the administration would close down the carnival just because I had a wild ride on The Snake last night? They don't even know about it. I don't know how it happened, or why, so what would I tell the dean?" Her eyes returned to Garth's face. "Is that what you wanted? For the carnival to be shut down?"

He hadn't been expecting that. "What? Why would I want that?"

Eve shrugged.

"Don't *do* that!" he yelled, startling her. "Don't say a stupid thing like that and then shrug when I ask you why you said it. Why *did* you say it? Why would I want the carnival closed down?"

Because you're still mad at the university and you have some kind of weird, insane notion that the full moon is helping you get revenge, Eve thought. But if it really *was* Garth, it would be very dangerous to accuse him. Aloud, she said, "Sorry. I guess I am still a little upset about last night. Forget it. Listen," turning to move away, "I've got to get busy. See you, okay?"

"Eve!"

She hurried away. She could feel his eyes boring into her back, but she didn't stop until she reached the cotton candy booth.

She didn't see Garth again the rest of that day.

The sky stayed a bright blue until late evening, no rain fell, and although the ground was muddy, no one seemed to mind. The crowd increased steadily.

At dinner in the food tent, Andie, Serena, Kevin, and Alfred all urged Eve to call it a day and go back to the dorm. "You look terrible," Andie said, "and everything's fine here."

"I'm not going until everyone else leaves," Eve said staunchly, slathering butter on a cob of fresh corn. She wasn't going to eat it. The thought of food made her ill. But she needed something to do, so she buttered the corn.

"You've done enough," Kevin said. "You deserve a rest. I'll take over here."

To her dismay, Serena suddenly began telling everyone about the defaced children's book. Why did she have to bring that up now? Eve wanted desperately to forget about it.

"Alfred has that book," Kevin said when Andie had finished. "Don't you, Alfred?"

Eve stopped buttering, let the cob of corn fall to her paper plate. It rolled to the edge and then lay still. "Alfred? You have a copy of *Moonchild*?" What was Alfred doing with a kids' book?

"Not anymore," he answered, stirring the pinto beans on his plate into a muddy mess. "I did have one. I'm doing my English term paper on children's lit, and Professor Mellon recommended that book. But someone stole it. While I was at the library, I think. At least, that was the last time I saw it."

Eve wondered if Alfred was telling the truth. Nothing in his perfectly angled face gave her a clue. He didn't look innocent, he didn't look guilty. He just looked like Alfred.

"You know, Eve," Andie said suddenly, "I actually wondered, just for a little bit, if maybe you were doing all of this stuff yourself."

Eve looked up abruptly.

A confused silence descended upon their table.

Eve sat perfectly still, her eyes moving from Alfred's face to Andie's. Her voice, when she spoke, was dangerously low. "Excuse me?"

Andie smiled lazily. "Well, after all, you *told* me you were sorry you'd ever agreed to cochair the committee, remember? No one actually *saw* anyone in the Mirror Maze, and no one actually saw anyone out here last night on the grounds, not even security."

Eve sat frozen on her bench. "What's your point?" she asked testily.

"Well, this afternoon when you were sleeping, the committee got together and talked about letting you resign. For your own sake. And it just crossed my mind that maybe that was what you wanted all along. I mean, we all know you'd never just quit. You're not like that."

No one said a word.

Eve was in shock. The committee had met behind her back? They had discussed asking her to quit? How *could* they? "You think I staged that stuff so it would look like I was in danger and I'd have a really good excuse to throw in the towel?"

"Andie," Kevin said sharply, "we decided *not* to ask her to resign. You didn't need to tell her."

"And I'm glad we decided that," Andie said earnestly. "I *said* I just thought about it for a minute or two. I even thought that maybe Eve was doing it without *knowing* she was doing it. You read about things like that sometimes. Never mind. You're not mad at me, are you, Eve?"

Eve was speechless. Whether Andie still thought it or not didn't matter. The whole insane idea was out there now, lying right smack on the table where anyone who wanted to could pick it up and toss it around, examine it, see if it was worth thinking about further. Alfred looked pensive, Serena looked confused, and Kevin looked embarrassed. It seemed clear to Eve that not one of them had immediately dismissed the idea as ludicrous.

Andie was her best friend! If *she* could think something so awful . . .

How many other people had thought it?

How many at the table were thinking it now?

Tears of anger and humiliation stung Eve's eyelids.

She got up and, without a word, left the tent.

The full moon, so bright in the cloudless sky that it cast a silvery glow over the carnival grounds, shone down upon her when she emerged from the food tent.

As she stood motionless, looking up, it seemed to her that the silvery beams radiating outward from the moon became long, grasping fingers, reaching down for her like the hands of a hungry predator, coming closer and closer . . .

Chapter 20

Eve shook her head to clear her thoughts. Then she decided to do what everyone had urged. She went back to her room, burrowed beneath the covers, and slept until Thursday morning.

"It's like you were dead, if you'll pardon the expression," Andie said as they dressed for class. "I talked to you when I came in last night, told you everything went okay, that the food tent didn't burn down and no one was poisoned or shot and we made money, but you didn't answer me. You must have been really wiped out. Feel better?"

Eve did feel better. She felt rested, and when she glanced out the window and saw nothing but bright sunshine, she made up her mind that that day would be better than the day before. Maybe Andie was right. Maybe her tormentor had crawled off to lick his wounds after she'd got away from him on The Snake. Maybe he'd given up.

"I think," she said as she fastened the barrette around her hair, "that tonight we should have some fun. We've all been working our little buns off this week, and we haven't had a chance to play. It's supposed to be a celebration, right? And that *is* a carnival, after all. We can let the townspeople on the committee do their bit, and the rest of us can go off and have a few laughs. What about it?"

Andie looked at her warily. "You're not still mad at me?"

Eve had forgotten. But now, in the bright light of a new day, it didn't seem important. "Well, I agree with you," she said.

"You do?"

"Yeah. You said you were crazy, and you're right."

Andie laughed.

There was nothing under Eve's pillow that morning, and nothing in her backpack that shouldn't have been there.

It's going to be okay, she told herself as they left the room, it *is*.

But she was wrong.

At first they did have fun. They ate hot dogs and cotton candy and Belgian waffles. They went on the merry-go-round with the little kids and made fun of themselves for doing so. Some of them rode the Devil's Elbow, some rode Hell on Wheels, and a few of them tried out The Snake. Eve wasn't among them. She couldn't even bring herself to go near it, and went with Andie and Serena to the fortune-telling booth instead.

Eve was careful not to show any scorn for the old woman in the tiny tent. Andie and Serena were fascinated, even though Andie's fortune told of a "dark past" and Serena's said that she would never marry, but would become very successful.

"If I'm that successful," she quipped as they left the tent, "I'll just *buy* a husband."

"So, what's your dark past, Andie?" Eve asked as they walked along the carnival grounds. It was dark out, but the area was well lit. Not that they needed much light, with the moon so bright overhead. "Murder? Arson? Insider trading?"

"Hmm. Have to think about that one. Probably the book I never took back to the library. Or Madama Siska, who knows all, sees all, hears all, could have meant the time I creamed Tommy Larson. He was teasing me and calling me carrot-top, so I punched his lights out." Andie shrugged. "I guess that's it for my dark past. Why didn't you have your fortune told, Eve?"

"The last thing in the world I want to know," Eve said dryly, "is what's in the future. I'm having enough trouble hacking the present."

"You look fine to me," Serena said blithely.

"Yeah, well last night, before I fell asleep, I actually found myself wondering if Andie didn't have a point. If I actually *could* have been doing those things myself. I don't know much about stuff like that, but I've heard about people who do things and don't even know they're doing them."

"Not you, Eve," Serena said as Garth, Alfred, and Kevin joined them at the Ferris wheel. "You're not the type."

Five minutes later, they were all sitting in the brightly colored cars suspended from the huge yellow wheel. Andie and Alfred were in the car above Eve and Serena. Kevin and Garth were in the car below them.

The night was warm, the darkness alleviated now by the bright-yellow lights encircling the Ferris wheel, and by the silvery moon overhead. There was a mild breeze, tossing Serena's long, blonde hair behind her as they rode up, up, up.

Eve had expected the wheel to stop when they reached the top. That was the most fun, stopping so high up and looking down upon the tiny ant-creatures scooting along the ground far below. Then making the car sway back and forth, harder and harder, until it seemed it would swing up over the top and do a somersault, spilling you out into the air.

But this Ferris wheel didn't stop when they were at the top.

It didn't even slow down.

In fact, it seemed to gain speed. The giant yellow wheel was already revolving faster than any Ferris wheel Eve had ever been on, and it showed no sign of slowing down.

No cars stopped at the top.

No cars stopped at the bottom, to let riders out.

The wheel whirled faster. The wind whooshed in their faces, stealing their breath, making their eyes tear. Screaming that had begun as delighted excitement began quickly to change to shouts of astonishment.

And still it gathered speed, this giant yellow wheel overlooking the Founders' Day carnival on the grounds beside the university. Faster, faster, spinning, spinning . . .

"Oh, God," Eve breathed, clutching the brass rail in front of her with both hands, "something's wrong!" She turned her head to see Serena's face a ghostly white, her loose, pale hair being tugged backward so hard by the force of the wind it seemed to Eve that it might be ripped right out of her scalp at any moment. Her eyes were red and watery, her mouth open in shock. Her hands, like Eve's, were frozen on the railing. "Serena!" Eve cried, "hold on! Don't let go!"

The screaming around them, shrill now with raw panic, increased in intensity and volume.

The wheel spun crazily, faster, and then faster still, as if it were trying desperately to escape its moorings and race off into the dark night.

Unbalanced by the unaccustomed, dizzying speed, the Ferris wheel began to teeter precariously on its base.

Chapter 21

Eve was so hypnotized by the incredible speed of the revolving wheel that when the unthinkable happened, she almost didn't realize it.

The wheel was by now spinning at such breathtaking speed that Serena, who weighed slightly more than one hundred pounds, was lifted up out of her seat by centrifugal force and tossed over the side as casually as someone might toss a used tissue or a crumpled piece of paper.

Still, she managed, with one hand, to retain a hold on the brass safety bar.

Eve screamed and lunged forward to help, as Serena dangled over the edge of the racing Ferris wheel.

"Give me your other hand!" Eve screamed, leaning as far over the side of the car as she dared. The wildly spinning wheel was already tilting dangerously, first to one side, then the other. The wind ripped at Eve's hair, her face, her eyes. Serena was no more than a blur in front of her. But she was still hanging on with one hand. If Eve could grab the other wrist, waving frantically in the air . . .

She grabbed, grabbed again, grasping nothing but rushing air. Then finally, her fingers closed around Serena's flailing wrist.

"I can't pull you up!" Eve shouted to the terrified girl, "but I won't let go! I promise you, I won't let go!"

Serena's eyes were wild with terror.

Eve hung over the edge of the car, its unyielding wooden side digging painfully into her stomach, the wind robbing her of breath, of vision. Her heart was pounding wildly in her chest. She was conscious of nothing except the need to hang onto Serena.

And still the wheel continued to spin out of control. It teetered dangerously on its moorings, as if it couldn't decide whether to stay or to go.

A scream, more piercing than the steady chorus of cries, rang out overhead, and a blur of green and blue, of flailing arms and legs, dove past, down, down, until it slammed into the ground far below. It bounced once, then lay still, a faint multicolored blotch in the carnival dirt.

Comprehension slowly forced its way through Eve's fog of agony. Someone . . . someone above her had been thrown out . . . someone hadn't been as lucky as Serena . . . someone had been flung to his death.

Eve clung more tightly to Serena's wrist.

Poor Serena slammed repeatedly up against the wooden car. Each time their car neared the ground Eve wondered if she should let her drop free. But the car swung back up into the air so rapidly, there was no time. Serena would probably have been crushed by the oncoming, speeding cars before she could roll to safety.

Eve, completely drained, hanging on now by sheer force of will, knew that neither of them could hang on much longer.

When the wheel started to slow down, she was afraid to trust her own senses.

But she wasn't imagining it. It *was* slowing . . . not quickly, but gradually, as if whoever was at the controls realized that a sudden, abrupt reining in of the renegade wheel could be disastrous.

So it happened slowly, so slowly that the hysterical screams continued until the wheel had come to a complete stop. Only then did the sound of hysteria, like the wheel's speed, diminish, becoming instead a soft, sickly chorus of gasps and groans of relief.

As the ambulances arrived, screaming onto the carnival site once again, each passenger's hands had to be forcibly peeled away from the brass guardrail. They had to be lifted bodily from the wooden seat and carried down the ramp to safe, solid ground.

Eve and Serena's car came to a rest midway to the ground. The minute the car stopped swaying, Eve used the last ounce of strength she possessed to haul Serena back inside the car, where she lay unmoving, scarcely breathing, her face completely colorless, until their car slowly inched its way to the ground and they were lifted out.

The minute her feet touched the ground, Serena fainted.

Chapter 22

There you are! See how much better everything works when you're right out there with nothing getting in the way of your beautiful rays shining down upon me? I could feel the power filling me up, making me stronger.

And listen, this was a very big deal. Couldn't have done it by myself. Too much even for me. Wasn't it fantastic? Have you ever heard such screaming in your life? Well, yes, I suppose you must have. But I hadn't. It was so exciting.

I felt totally invincible. So powerful! It was the most exhilarating experience of my life.

They'll shut it down now. They'll have to. And the whole, stupid thing will go down in Salem's history as one massive failure. She'll be held responsible, of course, she and the others. They all deserve it. Naysayers. Skeptics. Who are they to judge? Ignorance is no excuse.

I have to let her know why it happened. I

don't care so much about the others. Let them find out or not, it makes no difference. All I really wanted to do was punish them, and I've done that. But her . . . I want her to know. That's what she wants, right? She can't stand not understanding something. So all I'm really doing is giving her what she wants.

Of course once she knows, I'll have to kill her. That's no big deal. It's not like I've never done it before. There was my precious mama first, and then after that, there was Carolyn, my best friend in high school, who should have known better. Learned her lesson, didn't she?

This one will be a piece of cake. She doesn't have a clue. I don't even have to be careful around her, which makes it so much easier.

Ready or not, Evie, here we come!

Chapter 23

The Founders' Day carnival at Salem University was shut down the next day. The first thing Friday morning signs went up all over campus, warning people away from the site while safety inspectors from the state combed every inch of every ride, and the Ferris wheel in particular.

Eve's reaction was immediate when she heard the news. The carnival is closed, she thought grimly. Will he quit now? Was that all he wanted, to shut down the carnival? Or was there more?

She had a chilling feeling that there was more. That it wasn't just the carnival he was out to sabotage. And silly as it was, she couldn't help feeling that it just might, after all, have something to do with the moon. If that was true, this nightmare wouldn't end until the moon was once again no more than a tiny sliver of silver.

That could happen tonight. The moon could be full tonight.

"It had something to do with a cog," Kevin told her that afternoon. "The Ferris wheel, I mean."

They were sitting on the fountain on the Commons, trying to relax and recuperate from their harrowing ordeal. Three people remained in the hospital, recovering from injuries. Serena had been released, as had Eve and her friends.

All but one. Don, the young man from Twin Falls who had manned the dart booth, was dead, Eve had learned the night before. She was still reeling from the news.

"What about a cog?" she asked Kevin.

"They're saying someone fooled with one of the wheel's cogs. The controls slipped out of gear, and that's all she wrote. We were lucky, one of the inspectors was kind enough to point out to me. We all could have been killed."

Eve nodded silently. Of course they could have. And it was no surprise that the controls had been tampered with. Hadn't she known that all along? "Well, at least they won't write it off as an accident. Maybe they'll even get to the bottom of things. Some answers would be nice right about now. As for the carnival itself, it suddenly doesn't seem so important, does it?"

"Oh, I don't know." Kevin shifted on the stone wall. "We've still got the street dances in town, tonight and tomorrow night."

Eve would go to the street dance tonight. Why not? If she could survive the Ferris wheel, she could survive anything.

Andie and Eve dressed for the street dance in silence. All of campus had been unusually quiet all day, and Eve wondered if anyone could possibly have a good time at the evening's festivities.

So she was surprised when she did have fun.

She hadn't had a chance the night before to talk to Garth except to make sure that he was still in one piece. He was, and other than bruised elbows and knees, he had seemed fine. It would be nice to see him away from campus.

He was waiting for her in front of the post office when she and Andie arrived in town. Traffic had been blocked off at the bridge in the center of town, and a crowd was already milling about while the band, a group from campus, warmed up on their wooden platform above the street.

"I was afraid no one would show up, after last night," Eve commented, glancing around. "But," she added with false brightness, "there's no Ferris wheel here, is there?"

She danced with Alfred, who was limping

slightly, and with Kevin, who seemed preoccupied. He had been a good friend of Don's and he seemed to be taking the death hard.

Serena hadn't arrived yet. Eve wondered if she would come at all. Her legs had been so badly bruised, she wouldn't be able to dance.

It was a beautiful, balmy May night. The kind of night when nothing is supposed to go wrong. The sky was almost clear, with only a few clouds off in the distance, the breeze warm and gentle, the streets and buildings awash in the silver glow of the pumpkin-sized moon.

Alfred wanted to take her home after the dance. She said no, thanks, as she always did. He seemed to take it well. Better than usual. He just shrugged and said, "Later."

Eve was dancing a slow dance with Garth, when he reached up suddenly and released her barrette. Her thick, curly hair spilled onto her shoulders.

"Hey! What's the big idea?" But she wasn't really angry.

"Leave it," he said softly when her hands left his shoulders and flew to her hair. "Hair that pretty shouldn't be held captive."

Laughing, Eve thrust the barrette into her jeans pocket and went on dancing.

Freeing her hair freed something else inside of her. She felt, for the first time since her father had left the house, like *Eve*, instead of just Nell's daughter.

"Thanks," she said to Garth after a while and he must have known what she meant, because he just smiled and nodded.

She had not intended to be alone at all. She had planned all along to keep someone she trusted with her at all times.

But when Garth said, "Don't go away. Be right back. If we're going to keep dancing like this, we need fuel," and left her, she didn't go very far, didn't seek out another safe someone to be with. Garth would be right back. So she just backed up a little, into a quiet, dark corner in front of the drugstore, away from the crowd.

"Eve?"

Eve turned around.

Serena, pale and sweaty, her eyes glancing around nervously as she tugged at Eve's elbow, pulling her backward. "Don't let him see us!" she whispered urgently.

"Who?"

"Alfred!" Serena held out her hands. They were holding a plastic bag, and they were shaking. "I found something, Eve. I wasn't going to come down here at all tonight, my legs hurt so bad, but I found this, and I thought you should see it right away." She handed Eve the bag.

Eve opened it and peered inside. "What is it?"

"Darts. Look! The metal-tipped kind. A whole bunch of them. And an invoice. Alfred ordered them, Eve, on his own. His name is right there on the slip."

Eve removed the piece of paper. It was dark in the corner. She had to hold the paper up to the moonlight. Alfred's name was there, his signature. She'd seen it before, on all the cards he'd sent her. "I don't understand," she said, glancing up at Serena.

"All this time," Serena breathed, "all this time, he was right there in the house. Right there at Nightmare Hall! Down the hall from me. Why didn't I guess? I'm so stupid. There were all kinds of clues. I just didn't see them."

"You're not a detective, Serena," Eve comforted. "What else is in here? Where did you find all this stuff?" She began poking around in the bag, careful not to cut her finger on one of the dart tips.

"I was supposed to ride into town with Alfred." Serena shuddered at the thought. "But I knew I wouldn't be able to dance, so I went down the hall to tell him I wasn't going. He'd already gone without me. Never even told me he was leaving. I guess he just took it for granted I wouldn't be going, after last night.

Anyway, I was about to leave his room when I noticed the bag. It says, 'Foley's Carnival Supply' on the side, see there?"

Eve looked. There it was.

"And I thought, why would Alfred be ordering supplies for the carnival? I knew you'd done all that stuff. So I peeked. And there they were."

Eve pulled something rough and prickly from the bag, held it up to the moonlight, remembered the bewildered look on Alice's face as she was thrown to her death. "Burrs? These are burrs, Serena."

"He wouldn't have picked one from the roadside the day of the parade," Serena pointed out. "Someone might have seen him. So he must have plucked a bunch of them before that day, when no one was around, and kept them. And that's not all, Eve. It's so weird. I mean, I knew Alfred had a thing for you, but . . ."

Eve held her breath. *"What?"* she hissed.

"Your name is all over the place. Doodles, everywhere. Eve Forsythe, Eve Forsythe, Eve Forsythe. On notepads on his desk, papers on his bed, on his cork bulletin board. He's really nuts about you, you know."

"But . . . that doesn't make any sense." Eve rolled the burrs around in her hand. "If he's so nuts about me, why would he try to kill me?"

"Because *you're* not nuts about *him*. You know about guys like that. If they can't have you, no one can. What probably set Alfred off was seeing you with Garth."

Eve couldn't think. She was trying to, very hard, but she couldn't. Alfred? Well, why not? That made as much sense as anything else. And Alfred believed in all that parapsychology stuff, and had been annoyed when they'd all poked fun, especially her. It was very possible that Alfred believed the moon gave him special powers.

"Do you think this is enough evidence to take to the police?" Serena asked nervously. "Maybe we should go back to the house and see if there's anything else. But don't tell anyone we're going, or Alfred might find out. If he caught us snooping in his room . . ."

She wanted to go to Nightmare Hall? Just the two of them? Alarm bells went off in Eve's head. Something wasn't right . . .

And then she remembered.

The voice at The Snake had said, "I killed my beloved mother." She had heard that as clearly as she'd heard that he was going to kill her, too.

Alfred's mother wasn't dead. Eve had met both of Alfred's parents on Parents' Day. They had both seemed quite hale and hearty.

Serena's mother, on the other hand, *was* dead.

Serena was lying about Alfred. And there could only be one reason why she would be lying, and why she would have the darts and the burrs in her possession.

"Okay, Serena," Eve said calmly, "that's probably a good idea. We'll go to Nightmare Hall, just the two of us. We'll get more proof about Alfred . . . I'm sure there's more . . . and then we'll go straight to the police. But I left my purse over there on that bench," she pointed. "Be right back. Don't go away."

And she turned, intending to blend into the crowd before Serena could stop her, and find Garth and the others.

But she never got the chance.

Something came down hard on the side of her head, crashing into her temple, and the very bright moon and the black sky and the crowd and the music and the bench where she hadn't left her purse, hadn't even brought a purse with her, disappeared into a thick, velvety black void.

Chapter 24

Eve knew where she was the minute she came to. As groggy as she was from the blow to her head, she couldn't mistake that smell.

An attic. She was in an attic, with its strong scent of mothballs, cedar, and that musty odor that always collects at the very top of a house.

And she knew, too, with sinking heart, which attic this was. She remembered it from the tour that Serena had taken them on the night they came for pizza.

Nightmare Hall. She was in Nightmare Hall, in its dark, stuffy attic above the third floor. She remembered it well. Low, slanted ceilings, boxes and old furniture everywhere, garment bags on hangers, and low, squat windows on one side, leading to a rusty old fire escape. She couldn't see well, but reflected moonlight showed the white lace curtains blowing in the night breeze. The windows were open.

"Well, well, well, look who's up! Hi, there."

Eve was lying on the smooth, hardwood floor in the middle of the room. She pushed up on her elbows to peer into the darkness. Her head spun. When she looked up, she saw Serena sitting on a pile of boxes, looking down at her.

"The door is locked, Eve," she said with pleasure. "It's just you and me. Isn't this cozy?"

Eve sat up, leaned against the legs of an old sewing machine. "No, it's not cozy," she said coldly. "It's crazy! What are you *doing*?"

"Well, me and Moon up there," Serena waved a hand toward the window, "are teaching you a lesson. You made fun of us, Eve. You made fun of the power."

"I wasn't the only one. Lots of people did."

"That's true. And one of them, Alice, is dead, isn't she, Eve? And Boomer would have been, if that stupid doctor hadn't been there. And the rest of them got a lesson in manners last night, didn't they?"

Eve sat up straighter. "You were *on* that Ferris wheel! You knew something was going to go wrong with it and you got on it, anyway. You must have known you might be killed."

"Oh, no," Serena said calmly, "not me. I knew I couldn't die. I knew the Moon would save me. It's true, I didn't really expect to be tossed over the edge. But even when I was, I wasn't worried."

"You were terrified. I saw it in your eyes."

Serena laughed. "Well, maybe I had a little crisis in confidence there for a few minutes. I was *very* high off the ground, Eve. But then I remembered who I was and that nothing terrible could happen to me, and I wasn't so scared after that."

"Yes, you were." Eve's head moved, studying the room. Moonlight, the very "power" that Serena believed made her invincible, was also providing enough light to see by. And what she could see was that the only way out was through those windows. The thought of the rickety fire escape turned her stomach. But two things she was sure of: It *was* the only way out, and this insane girl in front of her, sitting casually with her legs tucked up underneath her, her hands behind her back, a lazy, smug smile on her face, intended to kill her.

There was absolutely no question about that in Eve's mind.

"Why do you want to kill me, Serena?" she asked, pulling herself to her feet. "I've never done anything to you. Okay, I made fun of those so-called 'powers.' But," she added gently, "you never told me you had any. How was I supposed to know?"

Serena's smile vanished. "Who said you could stand up? Stay right there, where you are. I didn't tie you up because you can't go anywhere with the door locked, but if you make one move . . ." She lifted the hands she'd been holding behind her to reveal a baseball bat. "I'll bash in your skull. For good this time."

"Oh, please." Eve took a small step sideways. "Don't be so melodramatic. It just sounds silly."

Serena jumped from her perch, her face contorted with rage. "See? See how you do that? See how you make fun of people, put them down so easily? You do it all the time, Eve."

Shaken, Eve stood perfectly still. Did she do that? Was she like that?

"*I* should have headed that committee," Serena shouted, brandishing the baseball bat perilously close to Eve's face. "Me! That's why I wanted it to be this week. The week of the full moon. Because I knew my powers would be strongest then. The Moon helps me. He helped me that first night, with my mother. A shadow moved across him and that was my signal that he was helping me. There'll be a shadow tonight, too. Any minute now. And I'll be able to tell when it happens." She smiled. "So will you, Eve, I promise you that."

Eve said nothing.

"You really should have picked me to chair the committee," Serena said. "I could have made this whole week the best celebration ever." Her lips twisted in a sneer. "Look how *you've* fouled it up."

"You're right, Serena," Eve said calmly, taking another step sideways. "But none of us knew about your powers. You should have told us. Then you would have been picked to head the committee instead of me."

The sneer deepened. "Ha! That's a big, fat lie! If I'd told you, straight out, you would have laughed your stupid head off. Stop patronizing me, Eve. I don't like it."

"How did you kill your mother?" Eve said.

Serena froze. "What?"

"I said, how did you kill your mother? You said that night on The Snake that you'd killed her, and I want to know how. It's not like I'm going to tell anyone. I mean, you're not planning on letting me out of here alive, are you?" She had said the right thing. It had shocked Serena, and she wasn't paying as much attention to Eve's movements. Another step, and then another, her feet sliding quietly on the hardwood floor.

"I . . . I *wished* her dead." Serena's voice

gathered strength. "That's how I knew I had the power. That was the first time I ever used it."

"You wished it?" Eve's words were heavy with skepticism.

"See? There you go again! Yes, I wished it, and it happened. So you can scoff all you want, but I wished it and it happened, and I wished it another time, too, and it happened. Carolyn was supposed to be my friend, my best friend, but she betrayed me, so I had to use the power on her. And it worked."

"Why didn't it work on me?" Eve was so close to the window now, the lace curtain brushed against her right arm. Serena didn't seem to notice. "I mean, I didn't die in the Mirror Maze, and I didn't die on The Snake. Maybe your power has blown a fuse."

Furious, Serena swung the bat. It slammed into Eve's wrist with a sickening crack. She screamed in pain, and bent double, clutching the injured arm. The blow shocked her. She hadn't been expecting it. "Oh, God, Serena, what did you do that for?"

"*Stop* making fun of me!" Serena screamed, her face a mask of rage.

When the bright light of the moon suddenly dimmed slightly, darkening the room, Eve couldn't believe it. There hadn't been a cloud in the sky. But now . . .

Serena noticed it, too. She ran to the window in the other end of the wall, and looked up at the sky.

When she turned around, she was smiling.

Beaming, really, Eve thought, she's beaming. There's a shadow on the moon and she sees it as a signal.

So, even though Eve was dizzy with pain and hadn't planned what she was going to do or how to go about it, when Serena, still smiling, lifted the bat a second time and broke into a run across the attic floor, headed straight for Eve, Eve had no choice. She dove out the open window and tumbled onto the fire escape.

It let out a screech of protest when her body hit the top landing, and groaned another as she tumbled heavily down the first three steps. The rusty metal stairs trembled with the sudden weight, and when Eve sat up and shook her head to clear it and looked up to see if Serena was following, her eyes widened with horror.

The bolts holding the ancient fire escape to the wall of Nightingale House were pulling loose. There were only four, giant-sized, fastened into the brick.

Only now they weren't fastened. Two of

them had already pulled loose and were hanging limply from the holes in the metal railing of the stairs. As the fire escape began to sway slightly, swinging Eve ever so gently, it pulled and tugged on the two remaining bolts which, Eve noticed with a sinking of her heart, were already loose in their holes.

Serena appeared in the window, her disheveled hair hanging over her shoulders. Her first glance was toward the sky, where the moon remained behind the shadow of a small cloud. Then, smiling, she looked down at Eve, crouched on the swaying iron stairs, her uninjured hand clinging to the railing, the other hand with its broken wrist lying uselessly in her lap.

"Don't come out here," Eve warned. "It's loose. Any more weight and the whole thing will go. Stay there, Serena, or we'll both be killed."

"Well, you will," Serena said blithely, swinging a leg over the windowsill, "but I won't. I already told you, nothing bad will happen to me. Especially now. Don't you see that shadow up there, Eve?" glancing up again. "The moon is full now, and that's when I'm strongest. Not only that, but there's a shadow, too. That's the signal it's ready to give me whatever I want, just like it did before. And what I want most,

Eve, is you dead. So that's what I'm going to have."

Eve had no choice. Later, she would tell herself that over and over again for a very long time, and others would tell her that, too. I had no choice, she would repeat again and again, until she finally believed it herself.

Serena, still armed with the powerful baseball bat, swung the other leg over the sill and prepared to drop down onto the fire escape.

And Eve shook it. With her one good hand, she gripped the railing and then she pushed her body against the railing with all her strength, sending the iron stairs swinging crazily to the right.

So that when Serena let her body drop, the fire escape that had been there only seconds before, directly beneath her feet, was no longer there.

She missed it only by an inch or two.

But she did miss it.

And went screaming to her death.

Eve, so sickened that she fell to her knees, caught only a glimpse of Serena's face as she plummeted straight down four stories.

But that glimpse was enough. What Eve saw was a look of total betrayal.

And she knew, as she collapsed in a heap on the metal stairs, that she hadn't caused that

look. It wasn't Eve, after all, that Serena felt
had betrayed her. It wasn't Eve that Serena
had expected to save her. And although it was
Eve who had swung the fire escape out of Serena's way, it wasn't even Eve she blamed for
her own death.

It was the Moon.

Epilogue

"Can't see the moon tonight," Garth said quietly into Eve's hair, which hung loose and full around her shoulders. "Too cloudy. Think that's why everyone's having such a good time? The music seems better tonight, people are laughing louder, talking more. Everyone seems more relaxed."

Eve lifted her head to look up at him. "That isn't because we can't see the moon, Garth. That's because Serena is gone." She rested her head against his chest again as they continued dancing on the main street of Twin Falls. "Poor Serena. She just totally lost it when her mother died, and no one ever even knew it."

Andie and Alfred danced by and waved. Although the moon no longer illuminated the streets and buildings, the crowd of dancers, and the river flowing off to the left, Eve decided Garth was right. Saturday night was much nicer than Friday. The air felt warmer, the breeze gentler, the crowd friendlier.

A deep pang of regret stabbed her. If only . . .

But what good did that do?

"I wish I'd known what was going on in Serena's head," she said quietly. "Maybe we could have helped her. It's so hard to believe she really thought the moon was guiding her, helping her."

"You heard Dr. Litton," Garth said, steering her expertly through the crowd. "Serena wasn't getting any power from the moon. It was her guilt that fueled her. She really believed she had caused her mother's death, and then later, that friend of hers. It's weird, but there it is. The important thing," he added, giving her a quick hug, "is that you're okay. The fire escape at Nightmare Hall isn't in one piece, but you are. Well, you will be, once that wrist heals," he said, looking at the cast on Eve's arm. "Think you can put it all out of your mind, just for tonight, and have a good time? And by the way, your hair looks fantastic."

"Thanks." Eve thought for a minute. The first thing she was going to do when she had recovered fully was change her major to graphic arts. She had survived this terrible week. She could survive Nell Forsythe's anger.

She raised her head again. "Yes," she said, "I can put it out of my mind. For tonight. But tomorrow, I need to think about some of the things Serena said up there in the attic. Maybe some of it made sense."

"Okay," Garth said agreeably. "Tomorrow, though, right?"

"Yes," she said clearly. "Tomorrow."

Return to Nightmare Hall
if you dare . . .

The roar of the motorcycle's engine is so loud, it can be heard from a great distance on this still, quiet spring night. An elderly woman named Myra pruning her favorite rose bush, the blooms pink with a faint hint of vanilla in their unfolding petals, lifts her head at the sound, and the straw hat she is wearing over her graying hair tilts slightly backward, exposing a lined forehead above slightly puzzled blue eyes.

Two houses up the street in the small, pleasant town of Twin Falls not far from Salem University's campus, the little Johnson boy, just turned seven and proud of it, fights to maintain his balance on the brand-new, shiny red and silver bicycle given him the night before at his birthday celebration. He loves motor-

cycles, and when he hears the unmistakable roar coming from somewhere behind him, he loses his concentration, then his balance, and topples off the bike. It rolls forward several feet, and then quietly lies down on its side near the curb, as if waiting for the little boy to catch up.

Although he has scraped his knee, drawing blood, the boy is too interested in the possible approach of a real, live motorcycle to cry. He pulls himself to his feet and stands in the middle of the street, eyes bright with anticipation.

It is twilight. The street, its neat white or brick houses and the fully leafed, large trees lining the avenue, are all bathed in faint purple shadows as darkness begins to silently swallow Twin Falls, gobbling it up block by block.

Any vehicle on the road at this hour is required to turn on its lights. That is the law.

But, though the roar of the bike increases in volume and intensity, the woman tending her roses and the little boy in the street see no sign of a light approaching.

If he had seen a light, the little Johnson boy would have moved out of the street and onto the curb to watch the motorcycle fly by, and would have counted himself lucky to see such a sight.

Myra, puzzled by the loud roar of the motorcycle when she can see no sign of the vehicle itself, rises to her knees and steps out into the street to peer down the avenue, thinking perhaps the roar isn't that of a motorcycle, after all, but someone's power lawnmower. She has seen the little Johnson boy in the street trying to ride his new bicycle, and wonders if she should call to him to move to the curb, just in case. But his parents might not like that, might think she's just being nosy.

She does see a light then, but it's confusing, because it's a double set of headlights, coming toward her end of the street. She may be old, but she knows perfectly well that motorcycles don't have two headlights.

Then what is that dreadful roar, so loud it could easily finish off what's left of her hearing?

The cycle appears out of nowhere, only slightly illuminated by the headlights of the car still some distance behind it. It is a huge Harley-Davidson with, it's true, no headlight at all, and only one rider. It swoops with a roar out of the purple shadows, catching the little Johnson boy by surprise. He waves, his eyes widening in astonishment, and then that amazing self-protective instinct kicks in and he dives sideways, out of the path of the oncoming motorcycle.

But the boy misjudges the distance between street and curb and as the rose-tending woman up the street watches in horror, the little Johnson boy misses the grassy area just beyond the curb, and falls too soon, his head slamming into the cement curb with a deadly thwacking sound.

Then there are three more sounds, each one breaking the early evening silence in a different way. There is the triumphant roar of the motorcycle as it races away. There is the shrill scream of Myra as she rushes across the street to aid the injured boy, and then, the agonized shriek of brakes as the approaching car tries desperately to avoid hitting her.

It fails.

The sound when the car hits her is quieter than the earlier sound of the boy's head thwacking into the curb. It is a softer noise, almost gentle as the sedan with the shrieking brakes collides with the woman, knocking her backward and under the car. It keeps going for a few more feet, dragging its victim along with it. When the car finally slides to a complete halt, the hem of a blue denim skirt clings to the bottom of the left front wheel.

Hearing the odd assortment of sounds from inside his house, the woman's husband rises from his leather recliner in front of the television set and hurries to the front door, opening it and calling, "Myra? Myra?"

About the Author

"Writing tales of horror makes it hard to convince people that I'm a nice, gentle person," says **Diane Hoh**.

"So what'a a nice woman like me doing scaring people?

"Discovering the fearful side of life: what makes the heart pound, the adrenaline flow, the breath catch in the throat. And hoping always that the reader is having a frightfully good time, too."

Diane Hoh grew up in Warren, Pennsylvania. Since then, she has lived in New York, Colorado, and North Carolina, before settling in Austin, Texas. "Reading and writing take up most of my life," says Hoh, "along with family, music, and gardening." Her other horror novels include *Funhouse*, *The Accident*, *The Invitation*, *The Fever*, and *The Train*.

NIGHTMARE HALL